Melanie Wilkins Culver

The Cost of Hope

For my mother, Deborah Ann Wilkins.

There's no way to be a perfect mother, and a million ways to be a good one.
-Jill Churchill

Chapter One

Alone outside in the cool, morning shadow of the wooden building, he sat with his back against the weathered, grey boards of the church. Under the ajar, west window, he could hear Reverend Kellam expounding upon the virtues of marriage and fidelity. Inside, the people of Pungoteague comfortably rested upon plank benches, warmed by their sense of fellowship and a wood burning stove. Outside, cross legged on the sunless ground, the desire to be inside among the good people of Pungoteague never entered George Davis Hickman's head. He had been sitting here, alone, under this window in the lee of the church every Sunday, absorbing the words of God, since he was old enough to walk the many miles to town.

The words of the Reverend sailed out of the window like cannonballs as George absently plucked newly sprouted blades of grass. Reverend Kellam's sermons were more rewarding when he wasn't so full of brimstone, but George reckoned there were some who might be in need of this message. He thought of his mother and wished yet again that she would join him under this window, but he had learned long ago that the answer would always be no. Elizabeth would only come to town out of dire necessity.

Across the churchyard lying at the perimeter of the pines and hickory, just beyond the headstones, was Honor, the pied hound who had taken George into his care some years ago. Honor didn't pant nor did he wag his tail when George looked up and met the unwavering gaze of the watchful dog. Today's vitriolic sermon made the Bluetick uneasy, and so Honor sat head up, still as a sphynx.

"The Lord our God ordains that man and woman should only lie together under the veil of holy matrimony, and then only for the express purpose of creating a new life!"

"Amen," echoed through the church and out the ajar window to land heavily on George where he sat out of the sun's reach. He sighed and stopped plucking grass blades.

"The fires of hell are the wages of the sin of fornication! So sayeth the Lord!" The Reverend Kellam's voice sent the birds flying from the trees above the tense hound as he sang out his favorite sermon, but Honor never looked up. His gaze never left George who likewise never lifted his eyes from the ground. They had heard this sermon before.

"And the fruit of unwed sin are equally damned, their souls barred from the gates of Heaven, destined to an eternity of agony and pain. Such souls were ne'er meant to walk this Earth and have been brought forth under the devil's watchful eye, belonging to Lucifer from their first breath!" Inside the church, the Reverend Kellam stopped to draw a much needed breath and his eyes cut cunningly to the west window. There was no echo of "Amen," just creaking boards as the Reverend's flock shifted uncomfortably on their benches. Outside Honor growled low in his throat. George didn't move.

"Let us pray," was followed by shuffling as the people of Pungoteague rose to their feet and began to dutifully deliver in one voice "The Lord's Prayer."

"Good people of Pungoteague, you may be seated. I wish to apprise all of some blessed occurrences before we disperse. Eugenia Rachel was born to the Custis family just this Wednesday past. Praise be to God for this wondrous event! We must all pray for the health of Eugenia and Mistress Custis in the days to come. " Again the amens, like a murmuration of swallows, echoed into the rafters and through the doors and windows.

"Further, William Miller wishes to announce the betrothal of his daughter, Mary Catherine, to Josiah Bayly, Jr," Reverend Kellam triumphantly shared. Mary Catherine looked up slacked jawed, William Miller looked down at the floorboards, the Reverend Kellam looked to the west window, and outside George closed his eyes.

5 days earlier…

Mary Catherine Miller, or Mamie as she prefered, sat next to George Davis Hickman down past the granaries on the marshy bank of the north branch of Onancock creek. The sun, free from clouds, was in their eyes to the west as it began the afternoon descent, but it warmed their faces while their legs, dangling in the cold tidewaters of the creek, tingled with pleasant, needling discomfort. The two sat in comfortable silence and watched the egrets fishing in the marsh across the way, while Honor lay with his back to them, monitoring the town of Onancock in the distance. Spotted turtles sunned themselves in the creek upon a fallen white cedar, saltmarsh sparrows competed with soprano melodies harmonious to the spring peepers' bass song, and George was thinking that it might just be a perfect day.

On Tuesdays, Mamie came to the sea trading wharves of Onancock with her father to sell what they could and buy what they needed from the little town of Pungoteague they called home. William Miller was a sailor and the bulk of his livelihood was made transporting folk in his bugeye to and fro across the Chesapeake Bay into the bustling harbors of Annapolis and Baltimore, but the fares were dwindling with the rising popularity of the newer steamboats. The sailor, to feed his family, took to fishing to narrow the gap and typically had striped bass and drum to sell on Tuesdays. He was down the creek at the wharf even now haggling with Seth Robbins over the price of croakers which had just recently completed their spring migration back to the bay. The sturdy sailor mistakenly believed his youngest daughter, Mamie, to be chattering about ribbons with young Louisa Guy who ran the register at her father's mercantile.

At mid day on Tuesdays, when his shadow disappeared, George would stop what he was doing, grab an apple and the Henry Rifle he had serendipitously found near his weathered shack in the woods of Cashville, and set out east through the sulfurous marshes and uncut groves of white cedar for Onancock, Honor on his heels. Skirting the eyes of the townsfolk, he'd wait patiently up the north branch hoping Mamie could steal away and would only abandon his vigil when the sun had sunk to the tops of the marsh reeds.

If Mamie could evade her father and that gossiper, Louisa Guy, to sneak away for an hour, their brief time together would sate George with a tranquility that would last him for days, making the tedium of the lad's daily life just about bearable. Mamie was a force, a tornado of a girl, and a warrior with a wicked sense of humor. She was also easy on the eyes with her long chestnut hair and those feline, blue eyes. She had been George's crusader now for nigh on a decade, defending him to all and sundry, and the two spent a disproportionate amount of time bickering about George's complaceny with his lot in life. The rest of the time he listened and chuckled while she poked fun at the various characters of Accomack County, but it wasn't the conversation that invigorated George. Her presence simply set his soul at peace.

If her father's watchful eye hobbled Mamie's escape from town, leaving George and Honor to wait alone for hours on the creek, the walk home to Cashville would become interminable, the shack would become a somber chamber of gloom, and a lingering discouragement would set in, shadowing him until the following Tuesday. Mamie was one of the few people of Accomack County that accepted George and treated him as her equal, and their short-lived time together was a consolation for the barren existence George knew he was meant to live. The girl was the color in his otherwise monochromatic life.

But today was not that day. Today, the sun was shining and so was Mamie. She splashed her legs, chattering on about Louisa Guy being sweet on Josiah Bayly and what a ninny the girl was for preening about in such an unladylike way. George thought to himself that some might at that moment call Mamie unladylike, kicking her legs back and forth with her skirt pulled up almost to her knees, her father for one if he were to catch them. George glanced back at Honor and was reassured that the hound still had his watchful gaze on Onancock. He then tried unsuccessfully to ignore the girl's lissome, bare legs, sneaking a glance when he dared.

"George, what do you think about marriage?"

George was quiet for the length of time it took a skiff to pass them on its way out to the Chesapeake Bay. "I don't think about it. There ain't no need." He picked up an oyster shell and skimmed it across the water.

Mamie, frustrated as always with the young man's acquiescence, reflected on the lack of emotion in his voice only momentarily before bitterly saying, "I think about it. I think marriage is a lifetime in the penitentiary unless you marry your best friend."

"Ain't many people lucky enough to do that."

"Well, George Davis Hickman, luck ain't got a thing to do with it."

"You thinkin' to marry, Mamie?" He was suddenly a little queasy.

"Either that or be an old spinster living with Mama and Father for the rest of my life," she said, voice a bit strident George thought.

"Don't figure it's in the cards for me, Mamie."

"Ain't nothin' worth havin' that ain't worth fightin' for," the girl said heatedly.

Because George wasn't certain why Mamie suddenly seemed so put out, they sat for a while longer in silence until she abruptly stood and said in a quiet voice, "Well, I have to start thinking about it. Mama and Father sure enough are." And with that she headed back to town.

While inside the well wishes celebrating the engagement resounded through the little church, George still sat without the warmth of the sun, looking at his paper patched boots. The Millers had indeed been thinking about their youngest daughter's future, but so had George. George had thought a lot about Mamie Miller and marriage in the past few days, but in the end there wasn't much to puzzle through. Little time passed before coming to the inevitable conclusion that he would very much wish to wed Mamie Miller and spend the rest of their days together in the sunshine, but this was an inconceivable hope.

George Davis Hickman was a penniless bastard, and an outcast. He was the unfortunate result of an unholy union as the Reverend Kellam liked to periodically remind the townsfolk of

Pungoteague. His mother was ruined in all the ways that mattered in the rural county of Accomack. One monumental mistake had cost Elizabeth Hickman her dreams, her security, the love of her family, the respect of the town, and, it seemed, her sanity. One simple mistake had sentenced her to years and years of misery, and that one simple mistake had also set her son on the path of isolation and hopelessness.

George nodded once in acceptance, and thought to stand when a wren, breathtakingly perfect, landed on his left knee. The brown and grey bird just gazed at George who very slowly and carefully pulled a loose thread from the cuff of his homespun, brown britches and laid it on his right knee. The wren looked at the thread, again at George, and then, like a dream, bird and thread were gone, off to build a nest, a home, a family.

George looked up to see that the sun had finally come over the top of the church and was shining down on Honor where he lay, still gazing intently at George. Time to go. As the Reverend Kellam came through the church doors, the townsfolk filing out behind him, he looked around the churchyard and was bitterly disappointed to find it empty. He turned, greeting his parishioners one by one until he got to Mary Catherine Miller who walked right on past his outstretched hand and out of the churchyard.

Chapter Two

Twenty years earlier...

Eleven years ago, Edward Henry Parker Hickman had been a destitute man. An illiterate farmer who couldn't grow weeds, he and his wife, Nancy, found themselves looking across an empty table at two starving children. Although Elizabeth, or Lizzie, was only 11 years old at the time and her brother, George W., a mere five, Edward Hickman made the decision to send his children out into service where they could work for their own room and board. With uncharacteristic wisdom he chose men with better farming skills than his own.

The Wise family farmhouse had thus been Lizzie's home for nigh on a decade, and she and the young, black slave, Sarah shared a corner of the well-ventilated attic and a bond closer than sisters. Every day, the two were up before the sun, starting fires in the iron stove and brick hearth, making wheat bread for the family to break their fast. Every winter night, Lizzie and Sarah dropped exhausted onto a straw pallet and curled up together under a castoff quilt, their combined body heat inadequate against the leaky rafters. During the summer the attic was stifling, the wet air heavy to breathe, and the two, lonely girls slept simply holding hands.

Although Lizzie had heard no word of little George W. since the day old man Levin Moore had come for him in a wagon led by two, equally ancient, draft horses, she was in the Wise kitchen stirring cabbage when a traveling man stopped to deliver the news that Nancy Hickman, her mother, was dead and buried in Mitchell's Hill Cemetery. Less than one year later, Farmer Wise, a hat and a letter in hand, found her in the kitchen garden behind the house and tentatively delivered the news that her father had remarried. Turning his broad brimmed hat in a circle he awkwardly waited for Lizzie to inquire about going home, dreading the answer he'd be forced to give, but Lizzie just went back to pulling wiregrass out of the midsummer sugar snaps. She knew the cost of hope.

Her new stepmother, Ann Stephens, was a far sight younger than Edward Henry Parker Hickman when at age twenty she consented to marry the forty-three year old widower. Truth be told, she hadn't even been aware of the existence of Lizzie or George until after she'd already agreed to the union and had to be reassured multiple times that they would not be rejoining the Hickman household. And so on the 30th of July, 1856, Ann Stephens wed Edward Hickman, now a moderately successful farmer, and immediately began the undaunting job of running his life. As the first order of business, she arranged for letters to be written by the Reverend Bonnewell informing the children of Edward that their father had remarried, was starting a new family, and that there was no place for them in the Hickman home. That done, she bought a mule.

So it was that late in June 1860 Lizzie was in the Wise kitchen stirring blackberries down for preserves and absently tending the two eldest Wise daughters as they played dolls under the kitchen table when Farmer Wise came in followed by a young man carrying a box of tools. The man was average, not tall or short, not thin or fat, not handsome or ugly, and Lizzie paid little mind as Farmer Wise took him through to the small bedroom in the back, momentarily returning alone.

"Well Lizzie, it seems young Benjamin Doughty is joining John Parker in the cobbling business and will be sharing his room as well." John Parker was not average. He was uncommonly ugly in nature and appearance and had been paying to room in the Wise household for the past year. Sarah in particular had reason to loath John Parker, a secret Lizzie shared, so another young man to contend with was not welcome news.

Lizzie didn't reply, just lowered her eyes and head in response and went back to stirring. She knew her place at the foot of the table with Sarah, and her opinion was certainly not welcome. Five year old Caty Wise, however, was not so reticent and popped out from between two chairs to share her displeasure,

"I don't like cobblers. John Parker said that me and Sarah were akin to lice. And I don't like to wear shoes."

With the patience and forbearance that had only encouraged the brazen child's sauciness, Benjamin Wise simply smiled vacantly and patted Caty's head saying,"Where's your mother dear girl? I need her to see to Mister Doughty."

Sarah's towhead popped out next to Caty's and she pointed out the door towards the barn. "Goats." She was only two.

More than satisfied that he had the situation well in hand, Farmer Wise rocked back on his heels patting his ample belly with both hands and then whistling a jaunty tune headed out to the barn to find his wife and turn the task over to her. The two small heads disappeared back under the table, and Lizzie returned to stirring blackberries. With little effort she put the nondescript boarder out of her mind and went back to daydreaming about a new Sunday-go-to-Church dress.

"I wonder if there's any bread left from dinner?" a voice startled Lizzie as she stared dreamily at the bubbling preserves seeing only grass green gingham.

Head bent, she looked up warily at Benjamin from the corner of her eye, "Under the towel by the sill sir."

Benjamin Upshur Doughty got his mediocrity from his father. John O. Doughty was 31 when Molly Folio decided that they would wed and up until that time had been contentedly coasting along with no real aspirations. Molly Folio Doughty however had enough goals for the both of them and settled into a pleasant life of nagging the indifference right out of John. Her endeavors paid off. John spent so much time at work, the townsfolk of Franktown, Northampton County, Virginia speculated on the origins of the ten Doughty children who seemed to appear one right after another. Between the caterwauling children and his pestering wife, labor became a welcome refuge for John who, in an effort to avoid going home, bought up the mercantile, the livery, and finally built a hotel. To his eternal befuddlement, he became a successful businessman.

Molly Doughty's imperious nature combined with her husband's sudden affluence afforded her the role of town matriarch, and all bent the knee, including her children. Now insisting on being called by her birth name, Mary, she held court from a Louis XV walnut Bergere wingback chair that she had imported from Philadelphia with the first profits from the mercantile, and when the livery purchase was finalized Mary celebrated by gifting herself a Henry Wilkinson silver plated tea service. From her wing backed throne, delicately sipping peppermint tea, she instigated and encouraged court intrigue while unabashedly playing her favorites one against another.

Benjamin Upshur Doughty was not such an anointed one. Fifth child of the brood of ten, he was nothing special in comparison to some of his more beautiful, talented, or intelligent siblings, a fact that his mother was quick to point out. To his knowledge, Benjamin had not once earned the approval of Mary Doughty although his pitiful endeavors were tireless. Making matters even worse, his father often seemed to forget his name, referring to him as, "You there…"

Because he was so seldom noticed unless being called to task, Benjamin was shocked when one day his father singled him out at the breakfast table by name. In between mouthfuls of eggs, John O. announced, "Benjamin, your mother has something to tell you," and went back to reading the paper.

Mary Doughty looked hard down her nose at John O. who took absolutely no notice and continued to read. She set her Newell Harding & Co. coin silver fork down in perfect alignment with her Waecstesrbach Blue FLow Ribbon plate and faced Benjamin.

"It's time for you to make your way in this world. To that end, there is a box of Cobbler's tools in the hallway which you will take with you tomorrow when you leave with the post on the way north to Accomack. You will take your room and board with Benjamin Wise and his family while you apprentice with John Parker. After one year, you will return home and wed Jane Bonnewell, and your father will give you a room in the back of the mercantile from which to work." Mary Doughty inwardly congratulated herself on her neat plans as she picked up her fork and returned to eating.

The daily breakfast noise then resumed around Benjamin who for his part simply sat back in his empire mahogany dining chair deaf to the din of silverware on china. Jane Bonnewell was a shrew, not quite to his mother's auspicious level, but she certainly had potential. There would be shrewish children, endless days of cobbling, and little joy, but perhaps also the opportunity to prove to Mary Doughty that he wasn't the failure she believed him to be. So full of bravado, he spoke loudly to the table, "I'll pack immediately." No one heard him.

Benjamin walked around the long, scarred, kitchen table to the sill of the open window and lifted the linen towel covering the remains of the Wise dinner. He carved off a thick slice of wheat bread and sat down at the end of the table near the hot hearth. Sighing, Lizzie stopped stirring, brought him the open jar of strawberry preserves, and poured him a mug of water. She had been thinking about lace trim on her new dress.

"Thank you Miss Wise."

Lizzie blushed, pleased that she'd been mistaken for something other than a scullery maid, and smiled prettily with eyes still downcast. "I'm Lizzie Hickman. I'm in service to the Wise Family."

Perhaps it was the blush on her cheeks or maybe the demure smile, but something in Lizzie's demeanor caused Benjamin to puff up just a bit. Swallowing his half chewed mouthful of bread, Benjamin stepped into the limelight for the first time in his life and made an inaugural attempt at gallantry. In a voice he believed to be quite charming, he proclaimed Lizzie too comely for servitude, and took a deep drink of water to get the wad of bread from his throat, watching the girl carefully over the rim of the mug. Although unsure that this was a compliment, Lizzie looked up directly into Benjamin's muddy brown eyes and let a dimple flash.

Spurred on by unforeseen success, he pressed on, all the while noticing her fine figure and burnished, brown hair. "Surely hands so delicate and fine were meant for piano playing or fine needle work?" And just like that, Benjamin thanked the stars for sending him to this backwater town in Accomack, because Lizzie laughed. The spell was broken only by giggling from under the table.

Nine months later...

"It's a boy."

Lizzie took the baby from her stepmother, Ann, in dismay, the weight in her arms concrete proof that this was not after all a terrible dream. She had somehow remained in obstinate denial of her ever more obvious state even though Farmer Wise, wife with arms crossed behind his shoulder, had with shame set her out of the Wise farmhouse. When her stepmother, Ann, had refused her entry to her childhood home, sending her instead to sleep in the barn with the animals, Lizzie had told herself that by and by her father would make room for her amongst his new family. Even when the labor pains made her believe she was being torn apart from the inside, she thought only of Benjamin Doughty and not the coming baby.

Lizzie had simply gone about life determinedly with no thought to tomorrow or the day after. She had milked cows, weeded the kitchen garden, and tended her baby sister and brother in return for the leftovers of the Hickman supper. In between she waited for Benjamin to walk up the dirt road full of apologies and remorse. What she hadn't done was muse over names for the infant, knit clothing, or give any thought whatsoever to where they would live. Lizzie had no swaddling, no blankets, and no plan.

When a disgusted Ann had put the baby in her arms, her first thought was not of the preternaturally complacent infant, but of Benjamin. Where was he? Lizzie was desperate to send word, sure that he would have a change of heart and rush to her side. Hadn't he doted on her all those months, sought her out for a private word, even sat next to her at the church social when he could have easily chosen another? Surely he regretted denying his involvement in the scandal, was sorry for having stood by while she was evicted from the Wise home. Hadn't he told Lizzie that he loved her that day by the creek?

Ann, her pink, calico apron covered with the mucousy gore of childbirth, stood sneering down at Lizzie, hands on her ample hips, and shook her cocked head knowingly. "He doesn't want neither of you, you little fool. You, Elizabeth, you made yourself easy pickins'. You ain't never gonna be good enough for the likes of him. Now, here I am, stuck with the both of you."

Lizzie looked at the baby so that she didn't have to look at Ann. The infant looked back with wide, dark eyes from beneath his dusting of black hair. There was a single moment when reality finally crystalized and Lizzie's spirit splintered, the infant just staring on complacently with that wisdom with which some seem born, as if he knew and accepted his life to come. When she started to sob, the child who hadn't cried even at birth simply gazed solemnly at the distraught woman and waited.

"What's his name to be?"

Tears and snot dripping off her chin, Lizzie looked down at the baby wrapped in a rough, old feed sack, the parasite that would forever more be her punishment, her burden to bear for her naive belief that she could be loved.

"Well Elizabeth, what's it to be?" Ann repeated, sharp and loud, her patience with the scandalous situation spent.

Just wanting more than anything in the world for Ann to go away and take this living, breathing penance with her, Lizzie whispered, "George Davis Hickman," set the babe down beside her in the hay, and rolled away from them both.

George Davis Hickman finally began to cry.

Chapter Three

May 2, 1882, Cashville, Accomack, Virginia

The sun was finally showing itself when George got to feeding the chickens the wild strawberries and worms he had spent much too long gathering the afternoon before. Mostly the birds fended for themselves, chicken feed being an ill-afforded luxury, but still George saw to the Dominique flock with tenderness. During the winter he regularly spent precious money on buttermilk, and he was careful to mentally note their favorite treats, diligently saving them scraps from his own meals. These chickens weren't for eating, granted George didn't exactly view them as pets, and although he collected the eggs the hens graciously laid, no chicken died by George's hand. There had been an occasional loss from a redtail hawk, but Honor kept away the fox and coons.

George sat down on a half rotted log near the dilapidated shack in which he and his mother, Lizzie, now dwelled, and immediately two, black and white, barred hens jumped up next to him. He chuckled fondly, and before he knew it the entire flock of twenty-three was at his feet, even the rooster who tolerated no one but George. The birds commenced a conversation clucking contentedly, and George simply sat and enjoyed a peaceful moment watching them scratch and peck.

The young man could relax a little now that the chicks hatched in April were finally sold and gone to the local farmers who had fought for the prized offspring of George's much admired birds. His Dominiques were known across Accomack for their hardiness, and while George might be an outcast to the community, it didn't lessen the value of his biddies. Now he and Honor could stand down, having diligently guarded the chicks for the past month against the myriad of ever present dangers. He thought the tidy profit just might get him through the winter.

George stood and stretched, yawning. He had been up from his straw pallet beside the cold fireplace hearth since well before the sun thought to join him. It was the same everyday. Lizzie would lie in their one bed, pieced together from scavenged wood, with her back to George and listen while he started the fire, cut a penurious amount of bread, and gathered whatever else he could find to break their fast. After he had swept the floor, set the meal upon the trestle table, and made bitter, chicory coffee, George would touch Lizzie gently on the shoulder. When she ignored his cue to arise, he would then eat standing up, leaving the one chair, a castoff from the Guy family of Onancock, for Lizzie who never rose to join him. His mother instead waited until he had finished his bustling and had left the one room shack, the very one that George, at the tender age of eighteen, had managed to provide.

When she was sure that George had gone, she would rise from the bed, never bothering to straighten the blanket, and sit down in the rickety cane chair that George had carried home to her the five miles from town. Lizzie would pick at the meager food, but she wouldn't cook, clean, or help with the animals. How she spent her time was a mystery to George as she rarely left the dark confines of the decrepit shack.

The rundown shanty and its two acres had only recently become their home. The first seven years of George's life had been spent living in Grandfather Edward's barn where he and

Lizzie were allotted the stall next to the milk cow. For over half of those years he had helped earn their keep by working alongside his cold, aloof mother in the kitchen garden or tending the livestock. In return, Ann allowed him to come to the house after supper for the miserly leftovers. Looking in the open door, he would see three young children, all close in age to himself, seated at the table contentedly eating their fill. Taking the meager scraps that were offered, he'd then head back to his straw covered home and a distant, resentful Lizzie.

The youngster often marveled at his two young aunts and uncle who lived in the house, ate at the table, and wore shoes, but he never needed to ask why he was different. His grandfather's wife, Ann, had educated him as soon as she believed him capable of comprehension, repeatedly declaring him a bastard, his mother a ruined woman, and both heathen in the eyes of the community. Grandfather Edward was often present for these life lessons but never intervened on George's behalf, only standing by silently with eyes downcast, so Ann's judgment was simply accepted as truth by the boy. As such, he didn't attempt to enter the house, made himself scarce whenever there were visitors, and never expected even the smallest kindness.

One morning, when George was barely seven, Ann awoke deciding she needed another milk cow and therefore the stall that was George's and Lizzie's home. Edward, in typical, obeisant fashion, immediately announced he was going fishing and left until dusk, leaving Ann to do her worst. By the time he had returned, his wife had seen to their eviction, and the two tenants were long gone, leaving only with the clothes on their backs. When Edward had dared to ask Ann of his daughter's and grandson's destination, he received a tongue lashing that had silenced any further questions.

For the next eleven years, George did whatever was necessary to maintain their existence, working as a goat herder for Mrs. Abby Custis, mucking stalls for Farmer Williams, and as he grew, tending the fields of Farmer Mears. He never made much, just a little food or a few pennies, and whatever he had George shared with Lizzie. For her part, she did little to contribute to their welfare. The one time she had chanced to gain a position in service, she simply walked away from her chores one day, never to return.

The two sheltered wherever they could, for a time in an abandoned fishing shack near Harborton, then a cast off two room house in Hacksneck, always in a place that George had, against all odds, scouted out. Everyday before setting off to work, the determined child would collect wood for a fire, haul fresh water, and tend the fishing net. Their diet consisted mainly of scraps from his employers and whatever he could forage on his way to and from his labors. Blackberries, blueberries, and raspberries thrived in the forests, and George knew of a grove of pecan trees. The fish were plentiful, and each autumn he carefully dried seeds from whatever he had managed to grow that year, usually just a few, poorly producing plants. Often out of pity, neighbors would consent to George collecting the half rotted peaches and apples from the ground in their small orchards. The young boy managed just barely to keep them fed.

A more maternal woman than Lizzie would have marveled with pride at not only George's determination and untiring motivation but also his inherent intelligence. Although he wasn't welcome at school and had never learned to read or write, the lad instinctively had a head for figures. No schoolmarm formally taught George to count. He reasoned it out himself, and when he went to town to buy their meager staples, he always handed the merchant the correct coins.

The meticulous math combined with his obstinate determination allowed George, at eighteen years of age, to buy the two acres on which the ramshackle, one room shack sat near the miniscule community of Cashville. Less than a town but more than a neighborhood, the grouping of homes sat squarely in the middle of Broadway Neck, a peninsula inhabited mostly by watermen and their families. To the east lay Onancock, to the southwest, Pungoteague. George's homestead was an outlier, much like George himself, and his closest neighbor was over a quarter mile distant, a fact that suited George just fine.

With the tiny homestead came Honor, the Bluetick Coonhound. No one could tell George from whence the dog had come, nor did it much matter. The two belonged to each other from the time they met. After squatting down, eyes to the ground as was his way, George allowed Honor to sniff him over and then waited for the dog to ask for affection. From that time on, the respect and devotion between the two was indestructible, and Honor took the role of George's guardian upon himself. In return, George was willing to die for Honor, his one, unconditional friend.

So on the cusp of manhood, George finally had a home. It mattered little to him that the one room construction seemed to lean a bit to the east and needed an overwhelming amount of repair. It mattered even less that the two acres weren't cleared. What did matter was that he was working for himself, and each morning he awoke with happy anticipation for the back breaking labor that day would bring. That first year he bought a few chicks and a handful of seeds, and by the following spring he had himself a flock of Dominiques and an acre of cotton planted. It hadn't hurt that he had found an old mule wandering in the redbud trees near the creek that second summer, and his luck held out when he stumbled over an old Henry rifle propped against a fallen tree only a month later. None of his neighbors laid claim to either, so George named the mule Lucky.

This spring was the third planting season for George, and he had spent the last two months with Lucky tilling the cleared acre of land and pulling stumps out of the other. He had invested in a used plow which had taken all he had saved and cost more than the actual land. He and Lizzie would need to live from the profits of the chicks and the sale of eggs, but George was undaunted. He planned to supplement their meager income by picking and selling wild blueberries next month, and blackberries the month after, something he had been doing for years. That should provide flour, salt, and a few other necessities, and if necessary, he'd find some odd jobs. He had hoped to buy a pair of boots for the coming winter, but that seemed a doubtful prospect. Out of necessity George had learned to patch his boots with deer hide and paper, so he'd have to stretch them another year.

After feeding the chickens, George and Honor set out to check his fishing net in Pakers Creek a few miles away, a little honey hole undiscovered by his neighbors. As they'd pass by Lemuel Jones' shanty, he figured on stopping to pay a visit and to give his friend a dozen eggs. Lemuel wasn't the only freed negro in the area, but like George and Lizzie, he existed on the fringes of society. The people of the area tolerated him and those like him, but they none were invited to church service or accepted through the front door of the mercantile. Because of this Lemuel was cautious and stayed mostly to himself, the better to guard the secret he kept. He could read and write, something most of the white folk in the area couldn't do, and if the people of Accomack County were to discover this, Lemuel was certain that nothing good would come of it.

Lemuel had in his possession a King James Bible, a mysterious treasure that George loved to touch and smell. Running his finger over the cover, he'd feel the old, cobbled leather and inhale the scent of the almost translucent pages as they fluttered through his fingers. He often found himself needing to ask God's forgiveness for the sin of coveting his neighbor's goods, but the pages were ephemeral, each filled with black markings that Lemuel could magically turn into righteous words, something the boy envied. The old, grizzled man could bring the Bible to life. George would lose himself for hours in the stories of the old testament, the Proverbs, or the epistles, which Lem said were letters written by various Christian folk, but today, George seemed distracted.

"You mind telling me why you lookin' sad as raindrops on a grave?"

George rubbed his hands over his eyes, sighed, and sat back on the rickety stool before saying, "Lem, Mamie's to marry Josiah Bayly. The Reverend Kellam announced it just yesterday at Sunday service."

Lemuel looked at George, but as usual, George didn't meet his eyes. He just looked down at the splintered boards of the worn table.

"I see. What you planning on doing bout it?"

"Nothing to do, I guess."

Lemuel cocked his head to the side and squinted hard at the young man. "That's it?"

Squirming a little on his stool, George shrugged, and said, "I know what I am, Lem, and that ain't good enough for the likes of Mamie Miller. She deserves better."

While George sat soberly resigned to a destiny dictated by small minded men like the Reverend Kellam, Lemuel began to build up a quiet fury at George's complacency, the people of Accomack County, and the general unfairness of the world. Because his skin was a different color, Lemuel was presumed to be stupid, uncivilized, and immoral. Because George's mother had committed a sin, George too would be punished. Both of the men were existing on the periphery of society, denied the rewards due them both for living a God fearing, righteous life. Neither of them believed there was any other choice for himself, but Lemuel wanted more for George.

"Now you listen here, George Davis Hickman! I been knowin' you for nigh on three years now. In all that time, I ain't never seen you say a harsh word to no one. I ain't never seen you miss the opportunity to do good in this here world. You a hard, hard worker. You ain't gonna tell me that Miss Mamie too good for you."

"Lem, it don't matter what you think. It don't matter what I think. Heck, it don't even matter what Mamie thinks. The only thing that matters is what her daddy, Reverend Kellam, and the rest of Pungoteague thinks.

"Well, boy, guess you must not love her much then. Might be she better of with Josiah Bayly, you not even man enough to fight for her."

George sat looking down at his hands which had closed into fists in his lap. Lem saw too and kept pushing. " A real man, he would ask Miss Mamie what it is she wants. If'n that's him, that man gonna go to Miss Mamie's father with his head up real high and ask for Miss Mamie. That's what a real man gonna do."

George stood up suddenly from the table, no longer complacent and accepting, no longer in control of the words coming from his mouth, and the stool fell over as he raised his voice to Lemuel in a rare fit of anger. "I know who I am, Lem. I know what I am. I may be a good man, a God fearing man, but you're an old fool!" And with that he stomped out. Lem sat back and smiled.

George blew out of the shack like a summer storm, thundering his feet on Lemuel's porch. As he marched across the yard, he was conscious of nothing but the old man's foolish words. Honor sprung up from where he was patiently waiting in the shade of a rhododendron and cocked his head as George set off down the deer path with Hell on his heels, the dog careful to trot several paces behind. They had traveled nearly a mile before George's pace began to slow and awareness returned. He stopped in the path and looked around at all the exuberant green that was Spring, and suddenly he could hear the birds singing again. When he looked down, Honor was sitting at his right side.

His anger was abruptly gone, and, instead, George was ashamed. As he and Honor trekked the remaining distance to Pakers Creek and the fish net, George thought about Lemuel's words and wondered if there was any truth to be found in his accusations. George had always known what to expect from life: isolation and a hardscrabble existence. A family of his own wasn't in the cards, and he had never hoped to live the life that all the other folk of Accomack were lucky enough to lead. George knew that there was a cost to hope, and he had never seen any point in paying that price. But a story that Lemuel had read from the big, black Bible a few weeks back suddenly came to mind. The Philistines challenged the Israelites, with whom they were at war, to choose a champion for hand to hand combat with their fiercest warrior, Goliath, reputedly a giant. David was the only Israelite brave enough to face Goliath, and armed with only a slingshot, he managed to bring the warrior down thereby, against unthinkable odds, winning the war for his people. The downpayment on hope was courage.

The generous fishnet had yielded two perch and a single striped bass which had ventured up the creek to spawn, a haul in excess of what George and Lizzie could consume. Taking the fish out of the net, he smacked their heads against a nearby rock, an act which invariably turned his stomach and caused remorse. This unpleasant task completed, George used his Bowie knife, another gift of providence found at that same fishing spot last autumn, to cut off the heads, a delicacy relished by Honor. He then made short work of fileting the fish before they went into the old strip of blanket he had fashioned into a sling.

A ten minute walk brought him to the Widow Bloxom's home on the outskirts of Onancock. The four room house was lavish by the standards of most Eastern Shore residents and had once been maintained with loving care. But that was before Southy Bloxom and his pungy schooner had gone down in Onancock Creek during one of the fast moving summer storms which would abruptly appear from the clear, blue sky. Now in most places the whitewash was faded to grey, the porch railings were loose, and oil paper covered two of the six windows. Widow Bloxom had a milking cow, a small kitchen garden, and a tabby tom cat, but she didn't have a husband, children, or an income. The fields lay fallow, and Apple scab had decimated the orchard.

As he entered the wiregrass covered yard of the neglected Bloxom house, he stopped and put his hand out palm forward to Honor who obediently sat. Last visit, Honor and Mouser, the tom, had engaged in an epic battle which had left Honor the worse for wear and squinting from his right eye for the better part of two weeks. Honor now seemed more than content to wait while George approached the house calling out in greeting. The Widow Bloxom appeared from behind the home, the tom cat at her side with hackles already raised. He trotted over to George and began to rub against his britches, eyes never leaving Honor, who was studiously examining the ground where he sat.

"As I live and breathe, it's George Hickman. Good day to you, young man."

George took off his hat, and, eyes to the ground, bowed slightly. "Widow Bloxom."

"What brings you, George. Been to town?"

"No ma'am. Been to Pakers Creek to check my net. Got a fish for you and Mouser's supper. A striped bass." The rockfish was the best of the three fish, the biggest, and George's preference, but it would also provide at least two meals for the Widow.

She clapped her hands together excitedly, "God bless you, son! Mouser and I were looking forward to another supper of fried corn pone tonight."

"That corn pone will go mighty fine with this fish, ma'am."

"George Parker, you are heaven sent. I wish I could pay you for this beautiful fish."

"No siree. I had extra. Ma and I can't eat all I caught, so's I thought of you. Right while I'm here, anything needin' doing?"

The Widow Bloxom shuffled her feet a little, hesitant. "Well, Betty's got a fevered udder. She won't let me strip the milk, and I'm just worried sick."

"I'll see to it, ma'am." George headed off towards the barn, the tom cat guiding the way, tail straight up in the air with delight.

The barn was in even worse condition than the house, and George made a mental note to return when he could shore up the beams. He remembered having seen the two story structure in the days of old man Southy when it had been neat as a pin. Now, like the house, it was weathered grey. The loft was filled with bats and barn swallow nests, the eaves with hornets, and rats ran in and out at their leisure despite the tom. The thigh high weeds were the perfect hiding place for the testy black snakes and occasional copperhead, and George worried about the Widow Bloxom's safety out here on her own.

Betty was tied up in a stall that hadn't been mucked for days, maybe longer, and the water trough had a green film across the surface. George untied the Jersey and led her out to the yard to graze as he set about mucking the stall. That done, George trekked over to the pump for fresh water and then led the cow back into the barn. After Betty had drunk her fill, George placed his hand on her withers and began to stroke slowly and gently. The cow turned her head and rubbed it against George, knocking him back a step, so he scratched her on her forehead between her eyes. He filled the hay basket with some dandelions and grass from the yard and sat down on a short stool at her udder.

George didn't need to guess which udder was ailing, one being much pinker and harder than the remaining three. When he put his hand to the painful teat, Betty stomped a little and looked back at George who braced to be kicked, but when all four hooves remained on the ground, he reached up and stroked her hind leg, cooing sweetly to the cow. Betty went back to eating her dandelions, so George tried again, and this time Betty stood stoically while he stripped the bloody, curdled milk from the infected udder. This would unfortunately need to be done daily until the infection had resolved, and George absently wondered how he would fit this into his daily chores. Mouser, sitting beside George's stool, looked up hopefully and mewed, so George cupped one hand under a healthy teat and filled it with milk for the purring cat.

When he had cleaned the bucket and refilled it with milk from the three, healthy udders, George walked up to the house and called for Widow Bloxom who came out the creaking door wiping her hands on an old, patched apron.

"Ma'am, you got any ginger, garlic, or goldenseal?" handing her the bucket of milk.

"Well, George, no ginger or garlic, but I got some goldenseal."

George nodded and explained the tincture she'd need to make and add to Betty's water trough daily to help the cow's infection. As he was speaking he took stock of the suns' whereabouts and decided it was past time to head on home, several miles yet facing him and Honor. If they hurried, he'd have just enough time to leave one of the perch for Lem as a peace offering. Putting his hat back on his head, he said his goodbyes to the grateful widow and whistling for his dog, they set off for home.

As the two followed the meandering deer path through the chestnut, holly, and paw paw trees, George thought eagerly of what tomorrow, Tuesday, might bring. While he worked, he'd made up his mind to speak with Mamie about her wishes, but he hadn't allowed his mind to wander further. George would cross that bridge if they came to it. Having made this decision, he began to jauntily whistle "Camptown Races" as they walked, and looking over, he noticed Honor wagging his tail.

When they reached the shack, the sun was setting, and the chickens had already gone to roost in their little, wood and tin coop. George checked on Lucky who was enjoying his day of leisure, and left Honor to guard the stead. Although welcome inside, Honor never set a paw in the shack but always settled at the stoop where he had the vantage point of the yard. His hound on sentry duty, George went in, taking his boots off at the door, to find the fire out and the room chilled. Lizzie was under the quilt with her back to him, so George said nothing. He lit a small fire and cooked the remaining perch, eating half and leaving half for the morning meal. He found a mealy apple with just the one wormhole to finish his supper, and crawled onto his pallet by the fire. As he pulled his buffalo hide over himself and closed his eyes, his last thought was of Mamie, and he fell asleep with a smile.

Chapter Four

Benjamin Doughty had lost sight of his wife and seven children in the dust and hustle of the Keller Agricultural Fair. Pulling a handkerchief embroidered with his initials from his breast pocket, Benjamin wiped his face while slowly turning in a circle looking around the Turlington Camp Meeting grounds for his brood. In truth, he cared little of his wife's whereabouts, but he enjoyed the company of his offspring and had just spotted a sweets vendor that sold the horehound candy so enjoyed by his son, Charles. The package of multicolored, satin ribbons he held would delight the elder girls, although the sixth, a toddler, would likely just soil hers with drool and dirt. At that thought, he smiled. Little Sarah was the apple of his eye, his spitting image with dark hair and brown eyes, and Benjamin considered it money well spent for a ruined ribbon that made her gurgle with glee.

When Benjamin had announced last week that he was traveling to the fair in Keller to purchase leather for his bootmaking, the children had all lobbied lustily to make the trip. Although a full day in the buckboard wagon bumping along the rugged, dirt roads was anathema to priggish Jane, the Doughty brood, who reveled in the time spent with their father, viewed the journey as an adventure, and, after all, the Keller Agricultural Fair was the biggest on the shore. His wife sent him a message with her narrowed eyes, silently instructing him on how to respond, but when Benjamin, already shaking his head to say no, looked at his ducklings dancing in place with anticipation, he instead declared, "Everyone must be ready by sun up on Tuesday next." Jane's cold glare was easily overlooked in the elated excitement of the children.

The nine of them had loaded onto the buckboard, the eldest six children packed into the back, baby Sarah on the seat between him and his sullen wife. Benjamin clucked to the two Percheron draft horses, Tuck and Joe, who took off like molasses, like Jane less than excited about their outing, and the Doughty's were off to Keller. They hadn't gotten two miles down the road when a skirmish over a doll erupted in the back of the wagon. Jane with eyes closed looked heavenward, but Benjamin chuckled. In a mock stern voice he vowed, "If you youngsters don't settle, I'll turn these horses around, and home we'll go."

The band of mostly merry travelers had managed to make Keller late that night only to find no room at the inn, the town of Keller bursting at the seams with folks from all over the Virginia peninsula. The children were undeterred by the inopportune circumstances, and when Benjamin hawed up in a grassy space on the outskirts of the fairgrounds, they fought for space under the wagon to bed down, excited about sleeping rough. The Doughtys had packed the wagon with blankets and quilts using them as seat cushions on the uncomfortable journey, and there was almost enough bedding to go around. After they had inhaled their supper of cold chicken and strawberries, which had made the trip safely under the buckboard bench protected by Jane's feet, the seven Doughty children laid their heads down exhausted but happy. Benjamin, who had unhitched the horses and led them to the livery, got back in time to see Jane, in the wagon with the two youngest girls, wrap herself in the last quilt and turn her back to

Benjamin. He chose to bed down on the soft grass next to the wagon instead, his coat his only comfort.

When Benjamin was stirred by the sun, he rose, noting the humidity already stifling the morning air, and immediately began counting heads. Charles, the only boy, was missing, but Benjamin wasn't worried. He knew where his lad was. For the entire sixteen mile trip Charles had spoken of little but the new racetrack that had been built for the Keller Fair just this year. He had droned on and on about his preference of trotters to pacers and their times around the half mile track, and, when Benjamin looked over his shoulder, he had noted with some satisfaction that Charles had literally bored his youngest sisters to sleep.

As Benjamin surveyed the awakening fairgrounds he saw the food vendors already setting up and knew breakfast wouldn't be a hardship. There would be cakes, breads, pickles, preserves, and canned fruit, and if he wasn't mistaken, the wind already carried the pleasant aroma of pig roasting on a spit. One by one the Doughtys arose from in and under the buckboard wagon, and Jane began tidying up her flock to the best of her abilities. For once the older girls, Mary Jane and Alice, seemed to care little over frippery (or the grass stains on their dresses), and together with the younger girls were impossible for Jane to corral. Resigned, she simply gave up, and the day at the Keller Fair began for the Doughty clan.

Now it was hours later, and Benjamin too had been unable to herd his flock. His family needed a Collie for heaven's sake. He thought of shouting out their names, but he knew his voice would go unheard over the blustering speeches of the stumping politicians. The livestock parade would be coming up, and he'd run his family to ground then. In the meantime, Benjamin planned to locate Thomas Teackle and purchase the tanned hides he'd need for the upcoming months. In the distance, he heard the starting gun signal the beginning of yet another horse race at the new track and could guess at least where Charles would be.

Benjamin found Thomas leaning against the side of his panel wagon in the shade of a hickory tree. The tanner had taken off the top panels of the wagon side to better showcase his wares which were piled high. As he approached, Thomas stepped away from the wagon and offered his hand in greeting. "Pleasure to see you here this fine day, Benjamin."

Benjamin managed not to grimace as the other man spit a stream of tobacco near his feet. "Indeed, Thomas, it is a pleasure" he declared, taking his hand. The foul odors of sulfur and lime wafted by Benjamin's wrinkled nose.

"So what are you after today, then?"

"Ten deer, 15 cow, and 12 sheep, my friend."

"I've got two untanned buffalo hides just arrived from out west, if you're inclined."

Benjamin considered, "And the cost of one of those hides? They'd have little use as boot leather, but my children might enjoy the novelty."

"$3.00 per hide, discounted for you. I'd ask $3.50 if'n it was anyone else." The tanner lied and spat again.

Benjamin knew he was being had, that $2.50 was the going price, but he thought of the excitement of his ducklings, especially Charles, when they saw the hide. "I'll give you $65 for the lot then, Thomas Teackle."

"Well now, I don't know that I can discount my wares that much, even for you Benjamin. I'd need $69 just to break even."

Benjamin understood this to be an exaggeration but also knew he'd need to bid at least $67 to strike a bargain so he offered, "$69, you throw in that second buffalo hide, and we've got ourselves a deal." Thomas spit on his hand and offered it to Benjamin, who with barely disguised distaste, took it and shook. Thomas Teackle might be a coarse man, but he had the best hides on the Eastern Shore.

Teackle turned his head to look over his shoulder and thundered, " George! Come here boy!" From behind the wagon appeared a young man, head down and wiping his hands on his ragged, brown, homespun britches. His linen shirt was yellow with age and bore the scars of many mendings. Although he did have suspenders holding up his britches, the lad had no coat, and the black, felt, slouch hat he wore had long seen better days. He stood looking down at his boots as if reading the newsprint that had been used to patch the holes, and shoved his dirty hands in his pockets.

As Benjamin took in the young man, George was what Teackle had called him, he felt gooseflesh inexplicably appear on his arms. He stood dumbly staring until Teackle, still looking over his shoulder, gave George his orders. " Go with Doughty here to fetch his wagon back to load the hides."

George nodded and looked for a millisecond at Benjamin before his brown eyes went back to his boots. In that minute amount of time, an odd sense of recognition washed through Benjamin, and his mind raced to place that face. After an awkward moment, he gestured to the lad to follow.

The two men set off across the fairground, George a step behind. They walked in silence, and when Benjamin slowed his stride to allow the young man to draw even, George curbed his step as well. For reasons he didn't bother to examine, this agitated Benjamin who finally stopped and turned to face his helper.

"We haven't been introduced. I'm Benjamin Doughty from Franktown," he said, extending his hand.

With a stunned expression on his face, the lad looked Benjamin directly in the eye for the first time, and Benjamin had to resist the urge to squirm as the boy's sudden, unreserved stare made him feel exposed. After a moment that lasted a year, the lad took Benjamin's hand and simply said, "George." When George's hand fell away, Benjamin felt a curious sensation of loss and sadness, and the confused man had to resist the urge to reach out and touch George on the arm, the shoulder, anywhere, just to reestablish that brief connection.

Instead, Benjamin turned and started walking again, waving to George to walk alongside. "So George, where's home?" Maybe that would explain where they'd met.

"Cashville."

"Can't say as I know Cashville. Is it near Keller?"

"About ten miles or so."

Benjamin, looking up, stole a sideways glance at the lad. "Up north, past Onancock?"

"Five miles west."

Not an area that Benjamin was comfortable thinking about. Before unbidden memories could overtake him, he pressed on. "Your father a farmer or a waterman?"

"Neither." Well this was like pulling teeth from a chicken.

"What trade does he practice?"

George, back to looking at his feet, muttered, "Don't have no pa." Well, that explained the poor condition of the lad's clothing. They walked on in silence for a minute or two, dust surging from the dry ground with each step. Finally, unable to resist his curiosity another moment, Benjamin asked if he had any other family.

"My ma. She lives with me on my stead," George said proudly, and the floodgate opened. The lad began to tell Benjamin the details of his home and acreage.

Benjamin was astounded at what George had managed to accomplish in eighteen short years: his own home and two acre parcel, providing for himself and his mother, all with only the most basic tools and resources. For Heaven's sake, the boy didn't even have a horse or a gun. He looked up at George admiringly. If only he had that determination and drive at eighteen. How different might his life have been?

When Tuck and Joe had been retrieved from the livery and led back to the buckboard, the two hitched up the horses and climbed up onto the wooden bench, George towering over Benjamin by inches. Though both had black hair, their complexions were different, George having the pale skin of black Irish descent while Benjamin had a swarthier look about him. Anyone looking at the two in profile, however, would have immediately noted the identical nose on both faces. They traveled back through the now mobbed fairgrounds, George peppering Benjamin with questions about his family, his boot making trade, and his home. How many children did he have? How long had he been married? What was his mother like? His wife? The questions came fast as if George was trying to learn everything he could about Benjamin in the brief time it took to reach the tanner's wagon.

Then the questions ceased, and George went back to staring at his boots as the three men loaded the cow, deer, and sheep hides. When Thomas heaved the buffalo hides out from under a pile of deer skins, Benjamin put up his hand to stop him. "One of those hides goes to your lad, George here, for his assistance today."

Teackle looked up, surprised, as did George, while Benjamin clumsily grabbed up the one buffalo hide and slung it on top of the others in the back of his own wagon. Turning to George, he again offered his hand which the boy now seemed less reluctant to take.

Thomas barked out, "Isaac Mears needs a hand with those deer hides, George," and with that the lad was gone. The loss of contact he had felt earlier was nothing compared to the wretchedness Benjamin felt now as he watched George walk away. Leaning slightly forward on his toes, mouth open, he resisted the urge to call out to him, to bring him back, but only just barely.

"Who is that lad, Thomas?"

"George Hickman from over in Cashville. I pay him to help on fair days. The Good Lord knows the boy needs the money. He's a bastard. No pa and his ma's not in her right mind." Teackle shook his head sadly. Pole axed with sudden clarity, Benjamin climbed up onto the buckboard and, in a fog, went to find his family.

On his way to the livestock parade, Tuck and Joe once again comfortable at the livery, Benjamin chanced upon his three eldest girls, Mary Jane, Alice, and Ella, fingering bolts of cloth at a fabric booth. Jane called out to her father as he walked unseeing through the throngs of fairgoers, otherwise he might have missed his daughters altogether. Rounding them up, they moved on to the parade where Jane had the three youngest girls on a blanket watching American milking goats prance by. Baby Sarah clapped her hands in delight when she spotted her father, and then held her arms out for him to pick her up. He put her up on his shoulders and she giggled happily. When the parade was over, and the last cow had strolled past, Benjamin herded his girls back to the buckboard and directed them to stay put. He headed off next to ferret Charles out at the track, planning for the two to bring supper back to the women.

When Benjamin and his son returned with a loaf of fresh bread, a jar of strawberry preserves, two more of canned peaches, and a blackberry tart, the children decimated the food like a plague of locusts. There were shouts of, "More, daddy, more!", and Benjamin, never able to say no to his ducklings, headed off to replenish the stores. Because he was smiling to himself and happy to be reunited with his family, he didn't notice the lad standing behind the tree. Long after Benjamin disappeared back into the dwindling crowd, the boy stood watching the Doughty family. He watched them eat the Shoo Fly pie and pickles that Benjamin brought back to the wagon. He watched them burn off the last bit of energy of the day catching lightning bugs in the dusk. He only stopped watching when the sun had set and the Doughty family had curled up in their quilts in and under the wagon, content, safe, and loved.

All the Doughty's were asleep by the time their heads hit the quilts, all but Benjamin. He lay awake staring at the twinkling stars, haunted by memories.

Chapter Five

George awoke abruptly, earlier than typical, knowing that the trajectory of his future would pivot on this day. Throwing off the buffalo hide, he rose to his knees and grabbed the poker to stir the cold embers. No fire. Tugging on his boots, he crept out the door of the shack to grab a stick or two of wood. Honor was sleeping on the stoop, and when George opened the door, the hound cracked one eye in annoyance. He carefully stepped over the dog, grabbed the wood, and humming "Polly Wolly Doodle" under his breath, went back inside to kindle the fire.

With the remainder of the perch left to warm on the hearth bricks, he neatly folded his hide and set to washing his face and hands with the water that he had hauled in yesterday. Still humming, he hung the filled kettle over the nascent fire and turning back to the room nearly stumbled backwards into the hearth. Lizzie, his mother, was standing at the table.

She stood in her undergarments with the quilt thrown over her shoulders, the messy braid of her dull, brown hair cascading over one shoulder. "There's a cost to hope."

George moved to the corner of the room where the broom was propped and began to sweep the floor. He said nothing in reply.

"We don't get to decide who we are, you and I."

George stopped sweeping and propped himself on the broom, looking at his mother. "I know who I am."

"Do you?"

"I'm your bastard son." Lizzy just stared at George, so he calmly went on. "I'm nobody. To you, to my father, to near about everyone."

She nodded. "That's right. Just like me. Nobody."

"I ain't just like you though. The price of hope maybe ain't too high for me."

"If you do this, you'll be sorry," she hissed.

George looked down at his feet shaking his head, still leaning on the broom handle. He looked up at his mother with pity in his eyes. "You know I'll be sorrier if I don't."

Without another word, Lizzie turned back to the bed and climbed in, cocooning herself in the tattered old quilt, back to George. He stared at her back for a minute, put the broom back in the corner, and, leaving the fish, headed outside.

Honor, oblivious to the exchange, got up off the stoop, stretching first his front legs, his tail end up in the air, then his back legs, toes pointed. Finally he shook himself vigorously and, morning ablutions done, sauntered over to the woods for a predawn constitutional. The chickens were clucking in their coop, critical of George's early start, but for once their complaints failed to amuse the man. He brought Lucky out of his lean-to shelter and tied him to graze near the water trough, giving him only a cursory stroke before he then set to his chores with determination, first tearing the weeds from the small garden by hand, then setting out with his hoe into the acre of cotton seedlings. He brooded over his mother's words and hacked angrily at the soil, stopping only for a ladle or two of water when the morning sun rose high enough for sweat.

For a time, he considered abandoning his plans. What Lizzie had said was true. No father, no money, no respect in the community. A nobody. This was not news. The knowledge of who and what he was had been ingrained in him since birth. Beginning with a mother who had never wanted or loved him, everyone, his grandfather's wife, the people of Pungoteague and Onancock, especially Reverend Kellam, had unerringly reminded him of his place in this world. Everyone, that is, except Lem, Honor, and Mamie Miller, the only souls who had ever treated George with a grain of respect.

A war waged in George as he hacked at the weeds in the precise rows of nursling cotton. He was not worthy of Mamie. She deserved better, but that should be Mamie's decision not his. Yet it wasn't Mamie's decision, was it? Her father had to allow their marriage, and George had no standing in the community of Pungoteague where the Millers lived. Mr. Miller would do as directed by the Reverend. The thoughts in his head came faster and faster, confusing George as he argued with himself. He was a good man, a hard working man, a God fearing man. He would make a home for Mamie that was worthy of her and the family they would create.

Family. He thought back to that day in June two years ago when he had watched the Doughty family laughing together as they chased lightning bugs. That was what he wanted, and he wanted it with Mamie. Closing his eyes, he could see laughing, barefoot children running up and down the rows of cotton while he worked and could hear Mamie's voice calling him for supper from the door of their farmhouse. He suddenly threw down the hoe, frustrated with the argument in his head.

The sun beat down from directly above George's hatless head, leaving no shadow. Time to leave for Onancock to meet Mamie. He looked around at the acre of cotton that he had worked for, fought for, and he suddenly knew that he could work and fight for Mamie too. He picked up his hoe and walked to the end of the row where Honor fell in behind him as he trod back to the shack. George found his blanket sling, picked up the Henry rifle where it was propped against the shanty, and replaced it with the hoe. Although his stomach growled miserably, he had no desire to see his mother, so he headed out without even an apple, his faithful hound at his heel.

As they walked cross country through the pines, across the cricks, and down deer paths, always skirting the neighbor's farms, George practiced what he'd say to Mamie, but the words didn't work, and in the end, he thought he'd be better off with short and simple. Something like, "Mamie, will you marry me?" George tore a leaf off a rosemallow bush as he passed, wadding it up and throwing it in frustration. He wondered if Josiah Bayly had plied her with pretty words, and, more importantly, if Mamie had liked it. He kicked a rock up the path as he walked.

Suddenly, Honor stopped and put his nose up in the air, sniffing rapidly. George stopped too and turned to look at the dog then up in the air in the direction of Honor's muzzle. Then he smelled it too. Smoke. Man and dog bolted for the clearing ahead where George could get a better look at the sky. Standing in the middle of the open space, he turned in a circle, eyes pointed upwards, until he saw the black smoke south of him. South of Savageville too, he reckoned as he looked east towards Onancock and Mamie. He made a decision and headed South.

The back of Obedience Parker's small house was on fire. Grease fire from the looks of the smoke, and thankfully it hadn't been burning long. Obedience was running towards the house with a bucket of water while Peggy and their four children stood in the yard wringing their hands and crying.

"No!" yelled George as he sprinted towards Obedience and the burning house. "Not water!"

Obedience was in a panic, but he stopped momentarily to tell George in gasping sentences that he'd poured three or four buckets of water on the burning stove. "The fire just got worse!"

"How did it start?"

"Peggy was frying potatoes in bacon grease. The potatoes started to smoke, and then it was on fire. She poured a pitcher of water on the pan, but the flames just leaped up and burnt her arm!"

"Obedience, no more water! We need dirt!"

"Have you lost your ever lovin' mind, George? Dirt?"

"We've got to smother the fire."

Obedience looked torn for a brief instant, but as he made a decision, he nodded, and turned to his family. "Edmund, Nathaniel! Get the buckets and the shovels. Fill them with dirt! Look sharp boys!" The two boys set to the task like dervishes, and the four set up an assembly line of sorts with George running in and out of the burning kitchen with each bucket passed to him. When the fire on the stove had finally breathed its last, young Edmund brought him an old horse blanket that George then used to beat the walls while the other three poured more soil on the small spots of fire that had sprung up in the grass around the back door of the house. For almost two hours they worked before the last of the flames was snuffed.

The four of them collapsed on the ground in the shade of an oak and little Bessie and Nan brought them ladles of water from the hand pump. After George had his ladle full of water, he looked over at Peggy whose left forearm had bubbled up like a boiling pot.

"Bessie, girl, run in the front door of the house and get some old linens." He stood, suddenly feeling lightheaded. When he had his bearings, he headed back into the charred kitchen. Luck was with them. At the back of the room, the only part of the kitchen not touched by the flames, was the Parkers' shelves of jars.

Looking through the preserves and pickles, George mumbled to himself, " Where are you. Come now." And then he found the honey, the glass jar warm to the touch from the heat of the fire. He picked it up and dashed back out to Peggy where Bessie was already ripping a sheet into strips.

"Mrs. Parker, let's soak your arm in the water trough." She looked fearful, but she nodded and followed him. Putting her arm in the cool water, she closed her eyes while a tear ran down her cheek but not a sound left her lips.

George nodded approvingly to her. "That's it, Mrs. Parker."

After many minutes had passed, George delicately patted her arm dry while Peggy stoically stood, eyes still closed.

"I'm sorry Mrs. Parker, but this is bound to be painful."

She nodded and opened her eyes to look trustingly at George. For once, George wasn't looking down, and instead returned her gaze with a reassuring regard of his own. He twisted off the lid of the honey jar and, using three fingers, scooped out a handful of the thick amber which he gently spread down Peggy's arm over the boils. He turned to Bessie who was standing by looking worriedly at her mother.

"One strip at a time, Miss Bessie," he said, smiling at the little girl. "You'd make a fine nurse." Bessie smiled shyly and proudly handed George the strips as he wound them round Peggy's arm.

"Now Mrs. Parker. You'll need to change this every day. Use a thick coating of honey each time."

"I'll see to it George," said little Bessie with no small measure of self-importance.

George smiled anew at the girl, and feeling lightheaded again, started back to sit under the oak tree with Obedience and the boys. Halfway across the yard, his vision became a pinpoint. He stopped and began to sway on his feet, hearing voices that sounded oddly far away and maybe a dog barking?

When George awoke, he was lying in the shade of a huge oak tree, his dog was licking his face, and, oddly, the Parker family from down in Savageville were all standing around him gaping anxiously. The smell of smoke in his hair and on his clothes triggered the memory of the grease fire, and he started to sit up.

Little Bessie, obviously taking her title of nurse to heart, sternly said, "Just lie back for a few moments, George. You've fallen out." She knelt on one side and put a hand to his left shoulder, and four year old Nan, not to be left out, quickly followed suit on his right. Peggy Parker handed little Nan a cool, damp rag for George's brow which the little girl managed to drape clean across his face by the time she was finished.

Just then his stomach let go an embarrassingly loud rumble. While the boys snickered openly, Obedience chuckled and asked, "George, when did you last eat?", and with that the womenfolk were off to see what could be salvaged from the kitchen.

George sat up quickly, protesting, "No thank you, Mrs. Parker. I've got to get to Onancock!"

"Nonsense son. You'll not make it to Warrington Branch, shape you're in," Obedience declared, obviously considering his word to be law. "Besides, least we can do is feed you, boy, after you saved our house."

Little Nan and Bessie came back across the yard at a full run, each carrying a jar, with Peggy following at a fast walk behind them with arms full. George sighed in defeat, scooted back to prop himself against the oak, and settled in to fill his belly. Honor draped himself across George's legs and wagged his tail.

On the north branch of the Onancock River, Mamie Miller stood tapping her foot impatiently. George was always here first, patiently eating an apple and stroking Honor's sleek, dappled coat. The sun was sinking, and soon she would have no choice but to sneak back into town. Now more than ever, she couldn't be caught with George. The whole of Accomack County believed her engaged to Josiah Bayly.

Mamie had dwelled on little else in the past two days other than how to explain this ridiculous misunderstanding to George. The Reverend Kellam, that snake in the grass, had been visiting the Miller house more than typical as of late, and she now understood why. Looking back, Mamie should have been suspicious when her father had sent them all, even Mama, outside to do chores while he and the Reverend talked at the table. William Miller waited on the Reverend Kellam himself, serving him coffee and whatever delicacies he could scramble up, something that should have alerted her to their scheming. Mamie had seen them through the window on one occasion, heads together, Reverend Kellam leaning in and gesticulating as he spoke, her father set back in his chair, looking down and shaking his head. But that day when William walked Kellam out to the porch, the clergyman had looked quite satisfied with himself.

The Reverend had made it his self-proclaimed mission to protect his flock from the likes of George and Lizzie Hickman, and he never missed an opportunity to school his parishioners in how such deplorables were to be treated by the righteous folk of their community. Just last month, Mamie had been in the mercantile in Pungoteague buying salt for Mama when the haughty minister had entered the store. Seeing Mamie at the counter paying for the purchase, the Reverend had casually mentioned to Mr. Scarborough that George ought not be using the front door of his shop, that he should be coming to the back door like the negroes. Mr. Scarborough had finalized Mamie's sale, handed her the change, and, turning to the Reverend, had politely asked how he could be helped that fine day. Mamie had stuck her nose in the air and left the mercantile with nary a word for the minister.

The ostracism of George Davis Hickman had been going on for as long as Mamie Miller could remember. She could recall being seven years old at a church picnic and witnessing George being told to leave in a voice resounding enough for all to hear. The young boy hadn't cowered before the threatening, black clad figure with the thundering voice. George had simply nodded his head to the Reverend Kellam, turned on his heel, and vanished into the trees. Mamie, holding her mother's hand for comfort, had looked up questioningly, but her mama had just put her finger to her lips and squeezed the little girl's hand reassuringly. The picnic that day had been a somber, joyless event for most all of the congregation even though the clergyman had belatedly done his best to liven up the festivities.

Not one of the Pungoteague community complained, however, at the Reverend's harsh behavior that day or any day since. The word of God was the law which governed their lives, and, as a man of God, the Reverend Kellam was never to be questioned, his behavior beyond judgment. Although the community's shunning of George made many uneasy in their hearts, they nonetheless accepted the minister's edict and obeyed like the good flock of sheep that they were. George, for his part, made this easy for them, as he asked for nothing and expected even less, accepting their denial with an inner grace that was uncanny in one so young.

All obeyed but Mamie. She, unlike George, was not full of grace, and openly questioned her parents' and neighbors' sinful behavior. She only stopped short of directly confronting the Reverend Kellam, because she knew her father would tan her hide. From that day at the church picnic, Mamie had appointed herself George's defender, a fact that was not lost on the minister. The more he preached against the sins of the flesh, the madder she got. The more she fought for George, the more he sermonized about the illegitimate spawn of sinful congregation. The tug of war had been going on for so long that it had become an amusement to the Pungoteague folk who chuckled quietly out of Mamie's hearing.

But there was nothing vaguely amusing to Mamie about the scheme that Reverend Kellam and William Miller had cooked up behind closed doors. Even her mother hadn't known and had argued with her husband, a sin in the eyes of God, against a match that would bring such unhappiness to her youngest daughter. In the end, she had gained no more ground than Mamie, and William Miller had slammed his fist down on the table, bellowing, "Enough!" But, spitfire that she was, Mamie was simply biding her time. The Reverend Kellam had won a battle, but she fully intended to win the war.

Mamie had no intention of marrying Josiah Bayly, that mealy-mouthed, clumsy fool. Her heart was set on George Davis Hickman, and she was fairly confident that everyone in Accomack County knew that but him. She had made up her mind to tell him today, to convince him to fight the Reverend Kellam and her father, but, for the first time, George hadn't been waiting. As the sun sank lower, Mamie's anxiety grew. He wasn't coming. Perhaps he thought she wanted to wed Josiah, and George had already given up without even trying. Maybe he didn't want to marry her after all. She wanted to scream and stomp her feet, but instead she wiped away an angry teardrop.

Mamie's fearful tears, however, soon gave way to her indignant anger, and although she could afford to wait a bit longer for George, she impetuously stomped back to town. There wasn't a soul on the face of the Earth with whom she wasn't currently infuriated: The Reverend Kellam, her father, the sheep-like people of Pungoteague, and, most of all, George Davis Hickman. The lot of them be damned!

He was going to make it. George and Honor had run the entire way from the Parkers' home in Savageville to the town of Onancock. Keeping his eye on the position of the sun, he pushed harder the closer he got to town. The smoke he had inhaled fighting the fire had shortened his breath, but he couldn't afford to pause to rest. George knew now what he was going to say to Mamie Miller, how he was going to convince her that he was worthy, and he had to make it in time. When he finally collapsed gasping for air and exhausted at their meeting spot, Mamie was nowhere to be found.

Chapter Six

George and Honor struck out for Pungoteague on the cusp of dawn. No sense in delay. Yesterday, standing in his field of cotton, he had made the decision to fight for Mamie Miller, and so battle he would. Although George was concerned for the lack of welcome he was likely to receive at the Miller home and worried that Mamie would somehow suffer from his brash and unannounced appearance, the die had been cast and he was determined to see this through, no matter the outcome.

The eight mile cross country walk took a few hours, and by the time the two neared Pungoteague the sun had climbed well into the blue, cloudless sky. His boots and feet had been uncomfortably wet from crossing the creeks snaking through the flat, wetland of west Accomack County, so he and Honor had loitered in a field of Virginia bluebells for a time watching the honey bees climb in and out of the indigo blooms. When feet and boots were again dry, he had picked a bouquet for Mamie, and man and hound had crossed the bridge over Taylor Creek bringing them into Pungoteague where George was no longer able to keep to the fields and groves. Instead he took to the rough-hewn road for all to see. When they passed St. George's Episcopal Church, he had to fight the sudden urge to turn and bolt for home, but George had crossed the Rubicon. There was no turning back.

Because the Millers lived just south of town, he walked the gauntlet through Pungoteague, his presence a poorly kept secret. As he passed the mercantile, Mr. Scarborough had come out to sweep the stoop and greeted him warmly as he passed. "Good day to you George!"

"And to you, Mr. Scarborough. I'll have some blueberries for you fore long, if you're interested," George had returned, full of false bravado.

Edwin Scarborough had never declined to do business with George, knowing that every penny was important to the lad's survival, and so he replied jovially, "The more the better, son."

Ahead on the opposite side of the street was Doctor Littleton's home and practice. The old Doc was sitting in a rocker on his porch, smoking his pipe. He waved in greeting to George as he passed.

"Beautiful day, eh George?"

"That it is, Dr. Littleton."

"Next time you have pecans, remember me, George. I've got a hankering for my wife's pecan pie."

"I sure will, Doc. You'll be the first." The wise, old coot had winked at George in reply.

George continued down the road waving to folks and returning greetings, Honor's tail wagging proudly like a banner. The entire town of Pungoteague must know where he was headed, and he guessed it wouldn't take long for the Reverend Kellam to know too. The closer he got to the Miller stead, the more he doubted the wisdom of this venture, and George realized his clammy palm was crushing the bouquet of bluebells. He forced himself to keep walking.

The Miller home was a modest, four room house set on a few acres of land which William Miller halfheartedly farmed when he wasn't out on the Chesapeake. Although the house could use fresh whitewash, Mamie's mama, Mary, had planted azaleas all along the front, and the pink was a stunning contrast to the white blooming dogwoods. The clothes line was hung with attire of all shapes and sizes, but no one was outside as George nervously approached the front door. Honor sat close at his right side as if to lend his strength as George closed his eyes, said a quick prayer, and raised his hand to knock.

William Miller opened the door. The tall, sturdy man stood silently eyeing George for a moment, and when he finally spoke it wasn't to welcome George to his home. "What is it you're wanting, Hickman?"

"I've come to see Mamie, Mr. Miller. Is she at home?"

"What business do you have with Mamie?"

"I'd like to speak with her, if you please, sir."

"About what?"

George, who had lowered his eyes the instant William Miller had opened the door, continued to stare at his boots as he considered his options. If he refused to tell Mamie's father what he had come for, the man might well close the door in his face. On the other hand, telling him the truth was no more likely to gain him access to the girl. He glanced up quickly into the scowling face of Mamie's father and just as quickly back down again.

"Sir, I've come to ask Mamie if she would ever consider becomin' my wife."

"You have some nerve, lad, thinking to ask her without speaking first to me," Mr. Miller spoke in a deceptively calm tone of voice.

"Mr. Miller, I only hoped to ask Mamie before troublin' you. I don't know that a marriage to me would even be to her likin'."

Mr. Miller, positioned squarely in the doorframe, prevented any view into the house, and George obviously was not to be invited inside. He knew from the man's posture and tone of voice what the answer was to be, but he had come this far and would see this through to the bitter end.

When the crusty sailor didn't reply, George risked a quick glance up and spoke quickly, the words plaintive, "I love Mary Catherine, sir, and I would be a good husband to her."

"Would you now, boy? You with not a penny to your name, a mother out of her mind, and a father who denies you? Tell me why you would make a better husband to my girl than Josiah Bayly?" As William Miller spoke, his voice went steadily up in volume until he was thundering, "Your own father won't have you. Why should I?" Honor growled low in his throat, and George rested his hand upon the Bluetick's head.

Although he had expected to be reminded of his baseborn status, the derision with which Mr. Miller delivered the blow caught George unaware and fractured his resolve. His mother had been right. He was unworthy, a nobody. Why hadn't he listened? George nodded his head, and looked up quickly to thank Mr. Miller for his time before going, all his fight gone. There standing behind William's shoulder was the Reverend Kellam, a smug look upon his craggy face. The clergyman, none to gently, pushed Mr. Miller aside and himself stepped into the doorway.

"George Hickman. The nerve of you, boy, coming to the home of this God fearing family, insulting them, debasing them with this proposition. You, a bastard, thinking that Mary Catherine Miller is within your reach? God forgive you, boy, because I certainly do not!"

George stood stoically, focused on a point of ground midway between them, and took the attack without flinching. Honor quietly bared his teeth.

"Be gone from this house! Be gone from Pungoteague! Take your ill begotten carcass back to that shameful whore of a mother. Do not dare to approach Mary Catherine or I will bring the law down upon you!"

George turned to go, and, as he did, he thought he heard someone inside the house sobbing.

Inside the Miller home, Mamie was sitting on her bed weeping, her Mama trying unsuccessfully to console the distraught girl. The gasping sobs were of the angry sort, and Mary Miller looked on worriedly. She knew her daughter well enough to know that these tears were only a harbinger of the storm to come, thunder and lightning sure to follow. She shook her head helplessly as she stroked Mamie's hair and braced.

When the Reverend Kellam had appeared on their stoop this morning, his pompous countenance had nearly caused Mamie to slam the door in his face, but her father was home, his bugeye in dry dock under repair, and so she didn't dare. She simply stepped back out of the doorway, and the clergyman had shown himself in, walking to the kitchen as if he owned the place. This time she went too, determined not to be left out of his scheming.

William Miller's greeting was lukewarm at best. The unplanned announcement Sunday past of Mamie's engagement had led to several days of misery for the man, with no one in his house having two words to say and his wife sleeping with her back to him. He glumly suspected this visit would lead to more woe, and so he only half-heartedly invited the preacher to sit. This time, when first Mamie and then Mary had entered the room, he didn't dare ask them to leave. The cat was out of the bag anyway.

Mary brought a cup of black coffee and placed it in front of Reverend Kellam, who, looking up at the woman, said, "Thank you, Mary. I take sugar."

Sweet as peaches, the woman returned, "I'm so sorry, Reverend, but we are plum out of sugar," something Mamie knew to be a bald faced lie, and although an apple pie sat plain as day on the sideboard, her mama didn't make a move to offer a slice.

The clergyman pushed the cup away to the middle of the table. He then turned to address William, pointedly leaving the two women out of the conversation. "Have you given thought to a wedding date?"

William Miller had hung his head for a moment, then looking wearily up at his town's shepherd, he said, "No, I haven't."

As the pushy clergyman began to speak again, "I believe we should start planning…", a knock had come at the door, and her father had arisen to answer, obviously grateful for the temporary reprieve. From her place near the door of the kitchen, Mamie heard everything. When the front door closed and the two men returned to the kitchen, they found the girl furious and crying.

No longer caring if she were punished, she looked an indignant Reverend Kellam right in the eye and hissed, "I'll not marry Josiah Bayly, and there ain't nobody in this room can make me, least of all you."

Man and hound retraced their steps up the dusty road through Pungoteague. Head down and shoulders slumped in defeat, George was unaware of the townsfolk, all yet at their posts. The housewives stopped hanging laundry and beating rugs to soberly watch as he and Honor, tail now down and still, plodded dejectedly by. Doc Littleton took his pipe out of his mouth and sighed sadly as he took in George's decimated bearing. He then looked across the street at Edwin Scarborough, and the two men shook their heads in disgusted agreement. All eyes followed the figure of the man and dog as they headed north, past St. George's, across the bridge and out of town.

George took no notice. He was focused on one thing only. Getting away. Getting home. Getting out of their reach. He wanted to be safe on his little plot of land, just him, his dog, his mule, and his chickens. He was desperate, almost frantic, though his body language gave none of this away. Outwardly, he might have appeared calm, but inside his heart was racing, and his breath was coming shallow and fast. When he had crossed the bridge over Taylor Creek and left the road for the camouflage of the trees, his breathing evened out at last and he allowed his shoulders to slump. He had to consciously unclench his fists, and the bluebells, still in his hand, had fallen to the ground. He never broke stride. Home. He had to get home.

When his land and shack were finally visible through the trees, George had expected to be relieved, to look with his typical satisfaction on the two acres, his cotton growing in the fields, his livestock, and even the rundown shanty. Instead, he noticed how dilapidated the one room house had become. There were gaps in the boards where drafts and vermin could sneak in. The oil paper over the windows and the missing shingles on the roof lent an abandoned look to the dwelling, and the wood siding had never seen paint.

The chicken coop was pieced together with scraps of wood and tin scavenged from trash heaps. The plow he had been so proud of yesterday was missing a blade, and Lucky deserved something better than the tiny lean-to enclosure where the mule sheltered. Heck, Honor didn't even have a roof over the stoop to protect him from the rain. George shook his head in disgust. Why had he been wasting time with frivolous dreams?

So this was the cost his mother had warned him of. The pipedream of a wife and family had cost him the satisfaction and pride he had felt for his accomplishments and his small farm. Time to pay the piper. He took the hoe that had been left yesterday propped against the wall of the shack and headed out into the cotton field.

Chapter Seven

Sunday, May 8, 1882

The Sunday service in Pungoteague came and went for the first time in ten years without George Hickman. He hadn't given up on God. No, it wasn't God's fault that he had been born a bastard, nor was it the Lord's fault that George had aspired for more than he was worthy. George simply had lost momentum, and he found himself that morning struggling against a deep, fatiguing inertia. He hadn't folded his buffalo hide when he arose and had forgone breakfast leaving Lizzie to fend for herself. George hadn't weeded the kitchen garden, walked the rows of seedling cotton, nor had he ventured out to check the fish net. He had taken care of the animals as his conscience had dictated, but afterwards had lost steam for the charted course of the day. He found himself sitting on the stoop with Honor blankly watching the chickens scratching and pecking in the grass.

George's mind had taken a divergent path this morning, casting aside the tunnel vision which typically propelled him through life. Instead of focusing on his goals, the young man found himself dwelling on the obligation he felt to care for his loveless mother, the unrelenting ambition to own this meager piece of land, and the deep yearning to be seen as a vital member of the Accomack community. His goals no longer seemed to be worth the effort. George, instead, arrived at the conclusion that he had been working only to feed his pride, a sin in the eyes of the Lord if ever there was one, and yet the alternative was bleak. He couldn't leave Lizzie to her own devices knowing his feckless mother would wither and die without his care, but he could accept this solitary path. Tomorrow George decided he would rise and get to business. Self-pity was as much a sin as pride.

Yet the young man couldn't help thinking of his father and the Doughty family down in Franktown. How happy they had been. For an instant, a sour resentment perfused his soul, and, looking up, he demanded to the overcast sky that God tell him why. Why didn't Benjamin want him? The love he bore his legitimate children was obvious to all, and yet the man was capable of abandoning a woman and child who desperately needed his name and care. Perhaps there was some quality inherent in George that made him impossible to love. That would surely explain the bitter emotion of his mother, the denial of his father, and the rejection of the people of Accomack. It would also explain why Mamie hadn't been waiting for him on Onancock Creek Tuesday past.

George looked down at his hand absently stroking Honor's sleek head, and an overwhelming adoration for the hound filled his heart bringing tears to his eyes. This dog would surely give his life for George, his love unconditional. God had given him Honor knowing the path of George's life and had taken pains to ensure that George wouldn't walk that path alone. As long as Honor breathed, there would be one soul that lived for George, and the man sent a silent prayer of gratitude thanking God for this gift, forgetting his anger moments before.

As George was wiping his eyes, Honor jumped up and began wagging his tail excitedly. Almost thirty seconds later, Lemuel Jones came up the path, a gnarled walking stick aiding his slow progress.

Standing up and brushing himself off, George called out in surprise, "Welcome friend! What brings you?" Lem had never before ventured out to George's stead.

"Making my way home from Sunday service, is all. Thought I'd take me a detour and say hello."

George walked over to the water bucket and offered Lem the ladle which the man took gratefully and emptied. As he handed it back, Lemuel cocked a brow and queried, "Your mama know you lettin' negroes drink from your ladle?"

"My ladle ain't it?"

"That it is," Lem smirked.

The two men walked over to sit on the rotting log. Honor, whose manners were as gracious as George's, caused some disgruntled squawking by chasing off the rooster who had been stealthily stalking Lemuel. The rooster's alarm had started all the hens in cackling as well, and this went on for a time. After the noise had finally died down, "What really brings you, Lem?"

Looking around and taking in George's home, Lemuel nonchalantly spoke, "Heard some talk this morning at church." George knew the man referred to the church the colored folk attended outside of Pungoteague. He just sat silently and waited for Lemuel to elaborate.

"Heard you made youself a trip to town Wednesday last."

George sighed, but said nothing.

"Heard the Reverend sent you packin'."

"Lemuel, what is it you're wantin'?"

"Just came to see how you's holdin' up is all."

"Just fine."

Still looking around, Lemuel offhandedly mentioned, "The garden needs weedin', and looks like you ain't been out to the cotton in a few days."

"Been busy is all. Plan on gettin' to it first thing tomorrow, but today is the Lord's day."

"That it is. That it is." Lem nodded, " You been busy workin' out how you gonna get around the Reverend?"

George looked down at his feet. "No, that ain't what I've been thinking about."

Again Lemuel nodded. "Talk is that William Miller said he wouldn't consider you cause you ain't got no daddy."

Exasperated, George jumped up and started pacing. "That's one of the things he said, but that's common knowledge, seems to me."

"Well, I seem to remember a conversation you and I havin' a year or two back regarding a cobbler you met at the Keller Fair."

Picking up a stick and winging it into the trees, "And?"

"Well, thought might be you'd be takin' a trip down to Northampton County."

George turned and looked Lem in the eye in disbelief. "Why would I be doin' that?"

"To see you daddy."

"For the love of all that's holy, man, why?"

"Cause, if you daddy claimed you, then maybe William Miller might see things differently."

George stood looking at his friend with his mouth agape. He finally closed it and resumed the pacing. Honor lay beside Lemuel, still sitting on the rotten log, and the two patiently watched George walk back and forth for several minutes.

When he finally stopped in his tracks, turning to face Lemuel again, he asked quietly, "You really think that would change things?"

"Dunno. Might though. I'm thinkin' you ain't got much to lose but a few days time. I can come tend you animals and look after you mama if needed."

"I don't know, Lem. That's a long walk to Franktown."

"What about the mule?"

George laughed, "Lucky ain't broke for ridin'. Sugar sticks, it's all I can do to get him to plow. Might be, I could pay to catch the post south though."

Lemuel nodded encouragingly, "Now you talkin'!"

"Truth is Lem, I don't know if I have the courage. Remember, I had the chance once before and didn't take it."

" A lot has changed since then, son."

George looked up from his feet into Lemuel Jones' eyes. "You're a fine friend, Lem. I am grateful for you."

"Hush, boy." Lemuel wanted to see George succeed. The man wasn't exactly sure why it mattered so much, but this desire had taken hold of him, and he planned to aid George in any way he was able. Slowly rising from the log, he grabbed his stick, doffed his hat to George, stroked Honor, and set off slowly into the trees.

George watched him go, then sat down in Lemuel's place on the log, and, staring off into space, spent the next hour deep in thought. When he finally arose to pins and needles in his legs, he had regained his determination and perspective. George had a plan. He would need a few days to attend to some details, but he thought he could set out with the post on Wednesday if all went well.

Looking at the shack grimly, he forced himself to walk across the yard, up the stoop, and in the door. Lizzie was sitting at the table patching a hole in the bed quilt, but she didn't look up when George entered the dim lit room.

"Would you like the oil lamp lit?" he ventured.

Without looking up, Lizzie mumbled no. George left the door open for light and leaning against the door frame, he crossed his arms over his chest and looked at his feet.

"I'll be leavin' for a few days come Wednesday. Just wanted you to know."

Lizzie finally looked up, and there was an odd look in her eyes. Was it hope, George wondered? Shaking off that senseless thought, he continued, "Makin' a trip down to Northampton County. Franktown. So likely won't be home til Saturday."

"You're going to see him."

Surprised, George nodded. "It's high time I officially met Benjamin Doughty."

Lizzie stood up from the table, quilt forgotten, and nodded eagerly. "It's time. Yes, it's time. Bring him home to us, George."

Looking back down at his feet, he told the delusional woman, "He has a wife, and seven children. Leastwise he did two years ago. Don't imagine he'll be comin' home with me, Ma."

She came around the table to George and put a bony hand on his shoulder. He forced himself not to flinch at her unfamiliar touch. As she spoke her eyes glittered feverishly, "When you tell Benjamin that I'm still waitin' for him, that I've been true all these years, he'll finally come."

George just nodded sadly. "Yeah, Ma. I'll tell him."

Lizzie smiled for the first time in George's life, and he could almost see the pretty girl she must have been. She clapped her hands together happily. "We'll be a family!"

For the next two days, George awoke to Lizzie bustling about the shack. George's heart ached to see her sweeping the floor, dusting the odd pieces of furniture, and mending her clothes. She combed her hair, bathed herself, and washed their scanty pieces of crockery. Worse, she hummed happily as she worked. He opened his mouth to remind her of the cost of hope, but shut it again quickly, leaving her to her brief time of happiness. All too soon, it would surely end.

That same Sunday evening, the Doughty family of Franktown was celebrating. At the senior Doughty home, Mary and John O. were hosting a soiree in honor of Benjamin who had just that morning been named Deacon of the Franktown Methodist Church. The guest of honor was looking quietly on from a corner of the room, reveling in the pride of his parents at last being bestowed upon him.

When Benjamin had returned home from Accomack County some twenty odd years ago, his mother had declared him a changed man, and he supposed that he had been. Gone was the irresponsible, bootlicking lad. What he had become instead was a somber, young man burdened by guilt. Heaven help, his parents knew nothing of the wreckage he had wrought while residing with the Wise family, and he told no one praying that gossip wouldn't spread its way south to Franktown. Nonetheless, he awoke every day that first year to the memory of his sin.

The day that Farmer Wise had been forced to confront Lizzie was a horror that played out recurrently in his head. The stout farmer wasn't jovial on this occasion with his wife standing behind him urging him on. He had called everyone to the kitchen, including Sarah, himself, and John Parker, leaving the children, thankfully out in the barn playing with newborn kittens.

"Elizabeth Hickman," he had abruptly challenged, "Are you with child?"

Although she didn't answer immediately, her hands had given her away as they drifted to the barely noticeable bump of her belly. Looking down, she realized what she had done, and when she gazed back up at Farmer Wise, there were tears in her eyes. She had then looked beseechingly at Benjamin, who, coward that he was, looked down at the wood planked floor.

The panic in her eyes further betrayed her condition to her employers, Mistress Wise demanding, "And who is the father of your child, Elizabeth?"

Again she looked pleadingly at Benjamin who had still refused to meet her eyes, but Mistress Wise didn't miss a trick.

"Benjamin Doughty, what have you done?" the woman had hissed. John Parker had smirked.

Like the craven he knew himself to be, Benjamin made his decision, and looking Mistress Wise directly in the eye, "I have done no such thing. I am not the father of Elizabeth's child."

The farmer's wife narrowed her eyes, staring hard at Benjamin who didn't flinch under her interrogating gaze. She then looked back to Lizzie, repeating, "Who is the father, Elizabeth?"

Lizzie was sobbing and couldn't, or wouldn't, answer.

Farmer Wise looked sorrowful when he spoke gently to the distraught girl. "You'll leave in the morning, Lizzie." The girl had nodded and run up the stairs to the attic where she remained until first light. She had been gone by the time Benjamin arose, and for that he was glad.

When he had ventured timidly into the kitchen to break his fast, Mistress Wise was waiting. "I am no fool, Benjamin Doughty. You are to leave as well. Please spend the day findin' other lodgings."

Almost five months later, living in the storage room of John Parker's cobbler shop, he had overheard John speaking to a lady of the community. Knowing that Benjamin was listening, the two had taken care to speak loudly and clearly as they discussed the birth of Elizabeth Hickman's baby boy just a week ago Monday. A boy. For a moment, Benjamin entertained a recurring daydream of marrying Lizzie. He liked her well enough, but it was the infant, his son, that drove the vision of him walking out of the bootmaker's shop to find the girl. On the heels of that reverie came a picture of his mother's face as he told her of his epic failure, and that was that. He would finish his apprenticeship as planned and return home to marry Jane Bonnewell. Benjamin would have to live with the guilt the best he was able.

The shame-filled man had fulfilled his mother's plans, married Jane, and become a cobbler in a room off his father's mercantile, all the while carrying the almost physical burden of remorse every step of the way. His marriage was stiff and cool, his labor unfulfilling, but happiness materialized when the children began to appear. He had found something he truly enjoyed and was quite good at doing. Being a father allowed him to temporarily forget the regret, so he set about making as many children as he could.

His burgeoning family led to Benjamin working harder and growing his business until he found himself opening his own cobbler shop down the street from his father's emporium. Mary Doughty had stopped belittling Benjamin, but still no words of pride or praise had left his mother's lips. As his business and family grew, he moved his brood into a stately home where they could all comfortably dwell, but all Mary Doughty had done was nod in recognition. The words of appreciation and pride had only come years later with the Methodist deaconship, and Benjamin was overcome that he had finally reached that long awaited milestone for which he had labored so long.

Mary Doughty stood in the center of the room tapping her Baccarat crystal glass with her expensive, silver spoon. When she had everyone's attention, she turned to Benjamin and actually smiled. Benjamin wondered if the smile was for him or for her audience, but he played along and beamed back.

"We are here to celebrate my dear son, Benjamin, now an elder of the church, a paragon of virtue, a quintessential family man, and a pillar of our Franktown community. Here, here!"

The cheer echoed throughout the room, and Benjamin found himself blushing unbecomingly. He stood and bowed to the guests, all the while knowing that the words his mother spoke, while pretty, were false, and that he was a sham. He made his way around the room, speaking with everyone and playing his part, but by the end of the night had come the stark realization that he had attained his life's ambition, and yet nothing had changed. The somber recognition that it was mother's love, not just her approval, that he had been after all along caused Benjamin to sink into a depression that was the antithesis of all this night had promised.

When he finally laid his head on the pillow late that night, his last thought before falling asleep was no longer of a bygone mistake and a son he didn't know, but of the worthlessness and futility of this life he had made.

Chapter Eight

Wednesday, May 11, 1882

The wainwright had been able to salvage the nave and most of the spokes, but, in the end, more than half the fellies had to be replaced. While the tradesman worked, Old Whit, the post driver, had taken the opportunity to catch up on gossip and beer at the Keller Inn leaving George to sit outside under a loblolly pine fidgeting and watching the descent of the sun. Although Keller was less than ten miles from Onancock, the starting point of George's journey, the post had stopped in Onley and Melfa, eating up valuable daylight. A mile or so north of Keller, a rut had shattered one of the post's wheels, and the wainwright and blacksmith had been working on the repairs for an eternity. At this rate, he'd not make Franktown until late tomorrow.

George fingered the coins in his pocket and did some mental calculations. There was precious little left from the money he'd made this spring selling his Dominique chicks, and now he'd have to stretch it even further. New boots had eaten up more than half his profit, and he'd impetuously splurged on new britches and a linen shirt thinking to appear respectable when he introduced himself to the Doughtys. Fortunately Old Whit had taken pity on George and let him on the wagon for only a nickel and some labor.

Two days ago, bright and early, he'd set off for Onancock to make his purchases which included the clothing and a little food for the journey. He'd fingered a new hat while his clothes were being parceled, but he didn't have the coin after purchasing the much needed boots. Setting the brown, felt Bowler back in its place, he'd turned to settle up.

Roger Ayres, the shop's proprietor, had jested, "You goin' courtin', George?"

The man had only been making casual conversation, but the question mortified the young man who was certain the gossip of last week's debacle had already spread like brushfire. Looking at the coins in his hand as he carefully counted them out, he said, "Takin' a trip down to Northampton for a few days is all."

"Business or pleasure?"

"Business I'd guess."

"Well you'll cut a fine figure, George."

"Thank you, Mr. Ayres," George murmured as he took his change.

George had already been at the boot maker's that morning having his feet measured so he headed over to the mercantile to purchase a few day's provisions. Henry Guy winked at him slyly as he approached the counter. "Welcome, George! Heard you're takin' a trip down south." No secrets in Accomack County.

Cringing, George picked out a block of cheese, a loaf of bread, two apples, and a jar of honey. "Yes sir, leaving on Wednesday."

"Safe travels to you, son."

By the time he'd picked up his finished boots and headed west towards Cashville, the whole town had seemed to know about his plans. Come tomorrow the rest of Accomack County would be in on the gossip too. He'd made the detour to Lemuel's stead to let his friend know he'd be away. The man had smiled and smiled until George, shaking his head, took his leave.

The next day had been spent tying up loose ends about the place, making sure all would be well in his absence. Although he had worked himself to near exhaustion, George had lain under his buffalo hide til the wee hours second guessing his decision. When he had finally arisen in the dark to head into Onancock where he planned to meet Old Whit, Lizzie had gotten up as well and lit the oil lamp. His mother had made the bitter, chicory coffee, poured two cups, and sat at the table while George put on his new boots. She eagerly nodded when George gave her last minute instructions on the care of the animals, her manic anticipation making her uncharacteristically amenable.

George drank his coffee in a rush, eager to be away from his crazed mother, hurriedly said his farewell, and headed out. Honor was waiting for him in the yard, already up, somehow aware of George's intentions.

"Not today, boy. I need you here lookin' after things." Honor's tail wilted down between his legs. George rubbed his head lovingly. "I'll miss you somethin' terrible."

Turning and heading off, he looked back to see the Bluetick slinking along behind him. He held his hand out, palm forward, and the hound reluctantly sat, ears flat back to his head.

"Please, Honor, stay." He could still hear the hound baying woefully a mile away.

He was missing his dog right now. Honor would be good company while he impatiently waited under this old loblolly. Stroking his silky ears, smoothing the coat down his lean back, knowing he was there, all would be enough to calm his frazzled nerves. He'd waste no time getting home to him, but in the meantime George stood up, stretched, and headed over to the Keller Inn to quench his thirst.

The inn, which served mostly as the local tavern, was quiet at this time of the afternoon, the farmers and tradesmen still making use of the remaining sunlight. The dark, cool room was empty save for a handful of men, two of which were sitting at a table in the far corner.

As George headed their way, Old Whit called, "Come on over, boy, and have a pint of beer. Nathaniel, bring my friend a round."

Sitting down, George nodded to the other man who extended his hand, "Alexander Cassatt."

"George Hickman."

"Pleasure, George."

Whit chimed in, "Alexander's down here strategizing for the Pennsylvania Railroad. They're thinking to extend the line from Pocomoke, and not a minute too soon, if you ask me. I'm ready to call this mail route quits. My arse can't take these roads much longer. Let the railroad do the work, I say!"

Alexander chuckled, "We've got to come up with a ferry across the mouth of the Chesapeake first. Don't get your hopes up Whit." The three men passed a pleasant hour pondering the logistics of laying track down the peninsula until the wainwright stuck his head in the door to say the wheel was back on the wagon and the horses hitched.

George reached in his pocket to pay for his beer, but Alexander stopped him. "I've got this gents. George, you've provided me with some valuable insights and earned your wages. You've been most helpful." The railroad man shook George's hand again as he and Whit headed out.

The post only made it to Painter that night, and, after offloading the mail, a local shopkeeper put them up in a backroom. George shared his bread, honey, and cheese with a grateful Whit who was sawing logs and farting not long after. Much like the previous night, George slept little. His mind wouldn't quiet as he considered all the potential outcomes of this impetuous endeavor. He was ready and waiting the next morning when Whit finally climbed up in the post wagon.

"Chawing at the bit, aren't ya son?" Whit chuckled. The grizzled, old fellow liked to play the fool, but he took the time to chat and gossip at every stop and precious little escaped him. Whit had never asked George why he was headed to Northampton County because he'd already put it together.

"Just want to tend to my business and get home again is all," George spoke quietly, all the while staring at his new boots.

This habit the lad had of looking down while speaking disturbed Whit. He had pondered it most of the trip but wasn't sure his advice was welcome. Deciding to take a chance, Whit said, "Some advice, son. Take it or leave it, your choice, but people hear you best when you're looking them in the eye."

George continued to look down, unsure how to respond. He eventually returned, "Just trying to be polite, Whit."

The grey bearded man laughed again, "You got it backwards, there George. Lookin' people in the face is a sign of respect."

"Maybe not in my case. Whit, you know my story."

The old man nodded thoughtfully, suddenly serious, "That I do, but let me tell you something son. If you think cause of that, you ain't good enough to look another man in the eye, then you are plain wrong. Any man who says otherwise ain't worth their salt." He flicked the reins, and the wagon began to roll.

About a mile down the road, Old Whit spoke again, "Here's an idea. Down here people don't know your story. Try it out on a few folks, and see how it feels. Might be, you see I'm right."

The wagon rolled into Belle Haven not long after, Whit hauled on the reins, and they hawed to a stop in front of the mercantile. Most small towns didn't have their own post offices so shopkeepers often tended the mail. George jumped down and trotted around to the back of the wagon eager to make the exchange and move on, all the while knowing Whit couldn't be rushed when he set to gabbing. When Whit pointed it out, he hauled the Belle Haven bag out and slung it over his shoulder, following the seasoned postman into the shop.

For the past three miles, George had been pondering the old man's earlier words and had decided to give it a go at the next stop. The worst that could happen? A belittling tongue lashing is all, something he'd endured many times before. He'd mentally rehearsed what he'd say to the shopkeeper, all the while looking the man directly in the eye, so when he entered the shop and saw that a woman was behind the counter, a young, very pretty woman, he'd stopped in his tracks. Old Whit turned and winked.

Whit sauntered gleefully up to the counter calling, "Morning Miss Lily. I'd like to introduce you to George Hickman."

The blonde beauty turned a radiant smile on the dumbstruck young man. "Pleasure to make your acquaintance, Mister Hickman."

Leaning an elbow on the counter, Whit turned to watch the show.

George cleared his throat and staring spellbound at the girl, said, "Likewise, Miss Lily."

Lily continued to beam at George, waiting for him to speak, while he struggled to find something, anything, to say. Finally, he stammered out, "You...you got a nice shop, here."

Lily giggled, "It's my daddy's shop. I'm just helpin' out. You helpin' Old Whit, here?"

"On my way to Franktown. Caught a ride with Whit." He slung the bag onto the counter, still staring at the girl. "Can I put this somewhere for you?"

"Well, ain't you a gentleman, Mr. Hickman? Come around the counter and I'll show you where."

While Whit grinned, George blushed but did as Lily asked, and when the bag was stowed away he grabbed the outgoing mail bag, slinging it easily over his shoulder.

"You sure are strong, Mr. Hickman."

"You can call me George."

Lily simpered, twisting a lock of blonde hair around her finger, George still gazing dumbly, until Whit broke the spell with, "Tell your daddy I was here, Lily, and say howdy for me."

"Sure thing, Whit. George, hope to see you on your way home from Franktown."

Still blushing, his eyes glued to the girl, George managed to get out, "Pleasure to meet you, Miss Lily." Turning quickly, he came from behind the counter and made tracks for the door, Old Whit strolling along behind, a big grin on the old fella's face.

When they got to the wagon, Whit nonchalantly noted, "Well, that went good."

The next stop was Exmore, a post office with a male postman. George breathed a sigh of relief and successfully managed to greet the man all the while looking him directly in the eye. Old Whit had been in no rush to be on their way and had wasted an hour jawing with the mailman and the sundry folk who had wandered in and out of the office. George, for his part, spent the majority of the time looking at his shoes and struggling not to fidget. He did, however, manage to meet the eye of anyone who spoke to him and reply in kind. As they left the post office, Old Whit slapped him proudly on the back, and they were off to Nassawaddox, less than five miles away and George's last stop.

After George had offloaded the assigned bag of mail and hefted out the outgoing post to the wagon, he went back inside to shake Old Whit's hand and thank him for his kindness. The older man walked him out, seeing him off on what Whit knew to be one of the most important ventures of George's young life.

The old joker was noticeably serious for once when he took George's hand, holding it for an extra beat, before saying, "Best of luck, son."

George looked him full on and nodded, his own eyes communicating that he understood Whit's words, said and unsaid, and that he was grateful to the old man.

Whit was starting to get a little choked up so he turned, shaking the lad's shoulder roughly, saying, "Off with you now. Daylight's wasting."

George laughed. Whit had never been worried about wasting daylight. He had no belongings to gather, so he simply turned and walked away, heading west towards Franktown.

Chapter Nine

Thursday, May 12, 1882 - Friday, May 13, 1882

At high tide, the briny water of Warehouse Creek often overflowed its mud marsh banks and flooded the road to Franktown leaving behind a stinking, treacherous quagmire. About a half mile outside of town, George could hear the cursing long before he eyed the source. Coming around the bend, a wagon came into view, the back end tilted at an angle which defied the laws of physics, a rear wheel half consumed by mud. Standing in front of an exhausted chestnut gelding, pulling at the bridle, was a short, rotund man with mud stains halfway up his body.

The sight was comical, but George suppressed his grin, hailing the distraught fellow as he approached the fiasco. "Howdy, Mister!"

The wee ball of man looked up surprised but unabashed at being overheard. "Thank Sweet Jesus! Damn but you are a welcome sight, young man!"

George stopped at the far edge of the mud pit and eyed the situation. "Looks like you're needin' some help, Mister," he called across the mucky section of road.

"That I am son. I'd be grateful for your assistance. I've been praying for someone to come along, and damn if the good Lord didn't sent you!"

Colorful way of praying, thought George, but he kept that bemusement to himself. He looked at his clean new shirt and britches, sighed, and sat to remove his boots. He rolled up his cuffs and sleeves knowing it was a useless endeavor and slogged into the mire. The sulfur smelling marsh mud sucked at his feet and he sank almost up to his knee with each hard won step. He grabbed the top sideboard on the back of the wagon, yanking back and forth, and began to work the nails loose. Pulling with all his might, the back end of the board came loose, and George abruptly fell backwards into the muck. Mud flew everywhere as he floundered.

"Oh, sweet Jesus," the ridiculous, little man had exclaimed.

Once he'd gained his footing, George easily freed the other end of the board and wedged the short end under the engulfed wheel, the long board pointing forward to the front of the wagon. After repeating the process on the opposite side of the wagon, this time more gracefully, he made his way out of the mud to where the pocket sized, butterball still stood holding the spooked horse's bridle.

"May I," he politely asked, gesturing towards the trembling gelding.

The odd, little fellow stepped back, and George walked up to the horse who was blowing through his nostrils. The horse tossed his head, his eyes rolling, but George just stood calmly until the exhausted animal quieted and brushed the lad with his soft muzzle, whiskers tickling. Only then did George reach towards the horse's head, not for the bridle, but to stroke him softly and gently. This went on for several minutes, George all the while murmuring to the steed and ignoring the little man who fidgeted and paced.

Finally, George said to the horse, "Ok, fella. Let's get you home," and gently took the bridle and gave a small tug. The horse came forward a step, tightening the braces, and stopped.

"Come on fella. You can do this." He pulled again, leaning his weight backwards a touch as he did. The third time George pulled, the horse pulled too, and the wagon began to move up the planks slowly but surely. Within seconds the wagon and horse were free of the muck, the chubby little man dancing joyously.

"Thank you, son! God bless you! I sure as hell can't thank you enough."

George stood stroking the horse as he turned and smiled shyly at the man. He walked around the edge of the mud pit and retrieved his boots, making a pitiful attempt to wipe his clothes clean of stinking, marsh mud.

When George returned, his laces tied together and boots slung over his shoulder, the man had clambered up in the wagon. He reached down holding out his chubby hand, "Reverend Frederick H. Myers."

George took the offered hand, looking the clergyman in the eye. "George Davis Hickman."

"Climb on up, lad. There's a warm bath and supper waiting for you, if you'll have it."

The sun was setting, he was filthy, and he wanted to make a good impression tomorrow, so George climbed up, and the exhausted horse plodded slowly towards Franktown. The Reverend Myers chattered on cheerfully for the next half mile. He was the leader of the Franktown Methodist Church. He had been to see an ailing parishioner and was returning home when his damned wagon got stuck in the muck. He hoped George liked oysters, because he was pretty sure the Mistress Myers was making fritters for supper. George just smiled and looked the Reverend in the eye every time the clergyman spoke, nodding when necessary.

The parsonage was a neat, two story home set next door to the Methodist Church, an imposing white washed structure on the Bayside Road. When they rolled to a stop outside of the small barn behind the parsonage, a tall, thin woman with a hawk nose and big feet came out of the kitchen door and put her hands on her boney hips.

"Frederick H. Myers, what in Heaven's name have you gotten yourself into now?"

The Reverend looked aside at George, still smiling. "That's my wife Beatrice. Sweet Jesus but ain't she a beauty?"

George guessed the woman was only an inch or two shorter than his own six foot height, but a half a foot taller than the Reverend. Beatrice was also painfully thin, but George reminded himself that true beauty lay within. Looking back at Reverend Mears, he answered solemnly, "Yes sir, she sure is."

George began unhitching the chestnut whose name he'd learned was Pete. After he'd rubbed him down and fed him his oats, old habits set in, and George found himself doubting his welcome at the parsonage. He was halfway across the yard, planning on simply saying goodbye and moving on, when Frederick stuck his head out of the back door yelling, "Hurry, lad. The bath water's hotter than hellfire itself!"

A short time later he found himself sitting at the kitchen table, clean but wearing clothes made for someone a foot shorter and twice as wide. Mrs. Myers was beaming down her beak of a nose at him across the table, refilling his plate every few minutes, and peppering him with questions. The Reverend Myers was bent over his plate, elbows on the table, shoveling food into his mouth at an impressive rate.

"George, what brings you to Franktown?"

Swallowing the mouthful of oyster fritter he'd been working, he replied, "I've got a little business in town."

"Who have you come to see?" She was kindly but with a tendency towards being a busybody.

George hesitated, then answered honestly, "Benjamin Doughty."

Beatrice clapped her hands. "Why, he's a deacon of our church! Did you hear that, Frederick?" The Reverend nodded vigorously and kept eating.

George braced for the obvious next question, but instead Beatrice tacked and began a new line of inquiry based on his people, his home, and his livelihood. George kept his answers short and offered as little information as possible without seeming rude. Beatrice seemed satisfied with the information she had gathered, while the Reverend Myers obviously was interested only in the last oyster fritter in the middle of the table. He'd been eyeing it for a minute or two, looking surreptitiously at the remaining food on George's plate and making calculations.

Putting the funny, little man out of his misery, George leaned back in his chair patting his stomach and groaned, "I couldn't eat another mouthful. What a wonderful supper, Mrs. Myers." Before he could get the second sentence out of his mouth, the Reverend Myers had speared the fritter proprietarily onto his own plate.

Beatrice smiled at the compliment, saying, "Well, I'll just go make up the guest room."

As she was pushing her chair back from the table, George began to protest weakly, "No, Ma'am. You and the Reverend have already done enough."

"But George, your clothes are sopping wet. I've rinsed them and hung them to dry. If you leave here in Frederick's clothes, you'll be the laughingstock of Franktown."

George looked down at himself and realized she was right. He'd not be going anywhere til morning, but that would give him a chance to nail the boards back on the clergyman's wagon. He also wanted to poultice Pete's fetlock. George had noticed some swelling while he was rubbing the horse down, probably from struggling in the mud.

He looked up at Beatrice and smiled, "Thank you, Ma'am, for your hospitality."

Frederick chimed in for the first time since supper had been served. "Beatrice is damned sure happy that you're here, George. We weren't blessed with children, so let the woman fuss over you a bit. It'll do her good." He winked at his wife who smiled lovingly back.

George slept in a bed that night for the first time, marveling at the soft sheets and the eiderdown pillow, and when the dawn broke, he found himself reluctant to leave the comfort of the thick quilt. But he rose and dressed in the Reverend's borrowed clothes, snuck down the stairs, and went out to take care of Pete after a quick stop in the kitchen for supplies.

Pete knickered in greeting to George from the comfort of his heavily bedded stall and was obviously pleased to see the young man, bobbing his head up and down enthusiastically. After making sure he was well fed and watered, George set about applying cabbage leaves to the horse's inflamed fetlock, securing them with scraps of linen. He made a mental note to explain the process to the Reverend before moving on. Standing up with the horse's head over his left shoulder, George leaned into Pete's withers, breathing deeply of his scent. Pete blew gently into George's hair, and the man momentarily forgot his fear and anxiety, feeling only peace.

"Thank you, Pete," and with that George made his way to the well to pump water for Mrs. Myers.

After a hearty breakfast of venison sausage, fried eggs, and fresh bread slathered with strawberry preserves, George fixed the wagon's boards, changed back into his own clothing, and set about thanking the Myers for their kindness. Beatrice seemed reluctant to see the young man go, and said a little hopefully, "If you're in need of a bed tonight after your business, George, do come back and join us for supper. We'll be having ham and new potatoes, if you're interested."

George thought that he might be inclined to enjoy one more night in that heavenly bed before heading home to Accomack County on the morrow. "I might just do that, Ma'am," and Beatrice beamed with pleasure.

George headed out, turning north on the Bayside Road towards Franktown. He didn't exactly know where he was going, but he figured he'd find Benjamin Doughty's shop easily enough. Franktown wasn't a backwater community like Cashville or Pungoteague, but it was no bustling metropolis either. There'd surely be a shingle to mark Doughty's shop.

George admitted to himself, as he walked down the dirt road to town, trying not to scuff up dust, that he hadn't thought this impetuous quest through in his typical single-minded manner. He'd been focused only on Mamie and his need for her. He hadn't considered where he'd sleep or how he'd get home, and so far it was providence that had met his needs, not careful planning. George chalked his luck up to God, never considering that it wasn't luck but his gracious spirit that people responded to in kind.

The morning was the best that May had to offer, and he wished Mamie was here with him to enjoy the warmth and sunshine. With her near he found that he felt lighter, that he could put down the heavy ache he unconsciously carried with every step. She made him feel normal, like all the other folk and not the outcast that he was, like anything was possible and within his reach. Mamie made him feel loved, and never having felt that from anyone except Honor, George was desperate not to lose the girl. If she were here with him now, George knew he could face Benjamin Doughty like David challenging Goliath.

As Franktown came into sight, George stood up straighter and squared his shoulders. He had committed himself to fighting for Mamie, and even though he had lost the first battle with Mr. Miller, he hadn't lost the war. The stakes were high, and he could no longer afford self doubt. Time to see this through.

Chapter Ten

Friday, May 13, 1882

Benjamin Doughty was nursing a hangover and feeling somewhat fractious. He knew he should be remorseful for snapping at little Sarah this morning, but the child had been tapping her spoon on her breakfast plate over and over until Benjamin could simply bear it no longer. When the lass had run crying to Jane, he had thrown his napkin down on his untouched plate, and fled that onerous house.

Now alone in the shop, Benjamin pressed his fingers into his closed eyelids, finding some temporary relief, although the headache came flooding back as soon as he released the pressure. He knew he needed to set aside the whiskey. This wasn't the first hangover he'd experienced this week. His epiphany at the party celebrating his deaconship had sent him into a profound depression, and the next evening, while feeling morose and melancholy, he had poured a glass of spirits. Because it dulled the edges of his pain, the next evening he had two. Even better. All too quickly, he found himself with a glass in hand from the moment he arose from the supper table until the time he went upstairs to bed, although last night he had never made it that far and instead ended up on the settee, sleeping in his clothing.

So far, Jane had not commented on this new habit and seemed to care little whether he joined her in bed or not. She had made it perfectly clear that eight children were enough and that intimacy was no longer desired. But his outburst this morning was likely to change her laissez faire attitude, and he dreaded returning home this evening to the disgusted look upon her cold, judgmental face. Perhaps he'd bolster himself with a small glass of courage before heading home.

Truthfully, Benjamin wished that he had discovered the blessed numbness of alcohol sooner. Perhaps his mother's barbs would have been less scarring, his father's indifference less wounding, and his wife less annoying. Perhaps he wouldn't have lain in bed at night feeling guilt and shame for the past twenty years. He thought of his ducklings and something similar to contrition began to worm its way in before he quickly shut down the unwelcome emotion, deciding that he was able to be both a good father and enjoy the medicinal effects of drink. Yes, he could manage that. He'd just drink a little less and avoid the thrumming head and bilious gut. Three glasses instead of five. Yes, that should do it. Not counting, of course, the one he planned to have here at the shop before heading home to that cacophonous house of children.

Benjamin sat down on the cobbler's bench and picked up the shoe last and hammer. Time to get to work. Mrs. Murray would expect her new kidskin boots to be done by this afternoon, and there would be hell to pay if they were late, the impatient woman. Just as he was about to get started, the bell over the front door chimed. Benjamin sighed and looked up. The sight shocked him, causing him to drop the hammer on his foot.

Gritting his teeth, he managed, "Hello, father." That witch of a wife must have gone straight to his mother since John O. had been in his shop only once before, that being the day it was opened.

"Benjamin." At least he got his name right.

"Come for a new pair of boots?" he attempted to appear lighthearted.

"Jane was by the house this morning to see your mother." He knew it.

Should he play dumb or get right to it? His father would be annoyed that he had been sent on this errand by Mary and Jane Doughty, so he'd best be to the point. " Yes, I overindulged a bit last evening."

John O.'s narrowed eyes suggested he wasn't buying it, so Benjamin quickly added, "I intend to apologize to Jane the second I return home this evening."

His father returned, "Your mother and wife are concerned that you've been drinking a great deal this week. Mary has asked me to inform you that you are to set aside the spirits. "

Benjamin's head was throbbing and he had no patience for this conversation or his mother's demands. He suddenly found himself with no desire to please her and, registering this, felt a newfound freedom. Freedom to do as he pleased instead of as Mary Doughty instructed. Freedom from his wife's disdain. Freedom from the uptight, puritanical rules imposed upon him by family and community. Freedom to speak to his father as he chose.

"Well, father, you've done your duty. You can report back to Queen Mary that you've been a good subject and done her bidding."

John's face reddened and his jaw clenched. "Boy, I'm not sure why you suddenly feel you can speak to me in such a way, but I'd remind you that I am your father, and I will not tolerate your insolence.

Benjamin simply shrugged and looked pointedly at the door.

"Remember that you brought this down upon yourself, you arrogant fool!" Fuming, the older man thundered out of the shoemaker's shop.

As the door slammed, Benjamin put his head in his hands, already regretting his impetuous behavior. He'd been on Mary Doughty's receiving end enough to forecast the suffering to come. He wished fervently that there was some way to extricate himself from his family and responsibilities, but that was just a pipe dream. He was stuck here in Franktown. He'd never be free of his mother or his wife. He opened the bottom drawer of his desk and pulled out the bottle of whiskey. Tilting the bottle to his mouth, he took a healthy swig, savored the burn, and set to work.

By the time George walked through the door of the shop, bell chiming his arrival an hour or so later, the bottle was more than half empty and Mrs. Murray's boots weren't done. Benjamin looked up, eyes bloodshot, ready for round two with his indignant father, but was stunned for a second time that morning when his visitor was not John O. but his bastard son, George. God was surely punishing him.

The boy had filled out in the two years since the Keller Agricultural Fair and was now more a man than a lad. George no longer stared at his feet, slump shouldered, but stood tall, eyes on Benjamin. His boots were new, and his clothes, although mud stained, bore no patches or rents. His son was a handsome man, black haired and dark eyed, and Benjamin felt instantly inferior despite his superior clothing, shoes, and upbringing.

As George moved into the shop, he took in the details including the half empty bottle of whiskey sitting on Benjamin's cobbler's bench, and his eyebrows arched in surprise. The hackles rose on Benjamin's back in response, the insolent pup, and he decided to make George work for this. "Welcome, young man. How can I be of service to you today?"

George cocked his head to the side in question. "You don't know who I am?"

"You must be new to Franktown. Haven't seen you around these parts before."

George took a deep breath, "We met at the fair a few years ago. I was workin' for Thomas Teackle, and I helped with your hides."

Benjamin pretended to consider it a moment, then said, "Ah, yes. I remember now. George was it?"

"That's right. George Hickman."

"Well, Mr Hickman, what can I do for you today?"

Benjamin was pleased to note the lad's discomfort. Good. He needed to maintain the upper hand. Then the boy blurted out, "I'm your son," and Benjamin knew that he would have no control of this situation.

"I know."

The silence reverberated as the two men stood sizing each other up. There was a time in Benjamin's life when he had longed for this moment, but for the life of him, he couldn't remember why. George stood waiting for some response from Benjamin, waiting to see in which direction the pendulum would swing. Already overwhelmed with problems, Benjamin just wasn't up to adding another.

"Why are you here, boy?"

"I need your help."

Benjamin laughed and picked up the whiskey bottle, taking a long pull before eyeing George. "If you're in need of assistance, you've come to the wrong place. You need to get on out of here before someone comes along."

George stood, feet wide and planted, and crossed his arms over his chest. "You can at least hear me out."

"Make it quick then. I've got a lot of work to do, and a family to return home to in a short time." The barb hit home, and for the first time, George looked at his feet. But just as quickly, he looked back up, defiant.

"I thought about all the questions I'd ask. Why you left me and Ma. Why you love your other children but not me. If you were ever sorry. But I guess I don't really care bout none of that after all. I just want one thing from you. I want your public acknowledgment, and you'll never set eyes on me again."

Benjamin slapped his thigh and laughed theatrically. Pretending to wipe a tear of mirth from his eye, he chortled, "You're plum crazy, boy. There's no way on God's green earth that I'd ever do that. No one knows about you, and there'd be nothing but problems if they found out. What do you think my family would say? I'm a deacon of the church, for Heaven's sake. I have a position and a reputation to maintain!"

George nodded his head slowly. "I expected someone like you to say something like that."

"Someone like me?"

"Someone who would turn a young girl's head, then leave her in trouble, and walk away from his own son. Someone who's a coward. Someone who's selfish and weak."

Standing suddenly and kicking the cobbler's bench aside, Benjamin got in George's space, but the boy didn't flinch.

"You know nothing about me or the choices I've made."

"You're right. I don't know you, but I've always wanted to. Until now."

"Then you'd best get a move on."

George obstinately said, "Not until you hear me out."

"Spit it out boy," Benjamin said as he righted the cobbler's bench and picked up the whiskey bottle off the table where he'd thankfully set it down. It was getting close to empty now, so Benjamin finished it off. He then forced himself to listen while George explained his situation. When he was done, nothing had changed. Benjamin still didn't care.

"I don't care about your problems, George. I have enough of my own. There is absolutely no way that I'm going to acknowledge you as my son." Benjamin stood as he spoke, teetering a bit. "I have eight children, legitimate in the eyes of God. I have a wife who is disgusted by me, and parents who have no pride or love for me. I toil every day at a job that bores me to tears, and I play the part of an upstanding business and family man to the community of Franktown. Where do you think you fit in to all this? What do I have to gain from you except more troubles?"

George looked sadly at his father. "I feel sorry for you."

Benjamin hissed, "I don't need your pity, boy!"

"No, but you got it."

"You get the hell out of my shop!" Benjamin slurred.

George nodded, turned on his heel, and left the way he'd come. Benjamin picked up the whiskey bottle for a slug, but finding it empty, threw it across the room where it shattered against the far wall. How had it all come to this? There was nothing in his life which made him happy, not even his children. All he felt was frustration and anger, melancholy and sadness. And futility.

George walked calmly down Main Street, head up and eyes forward. On the outside, he appeared composed and casual, but on the inside he was wild with desperation. A maelstrom of emotions was knotted in a choking ball in his chest, a knot he couldn't untangle enough to even name what he was feeling. He trod resolutely down the street until he was out of town, then veered off the dirt road into the trees until he was out of view. He sat down with his back against a hickory tree and began to sob in angry, frustrated bursts.

At first he wept for the end of a dream, a hope he had nurtured for twenty years. All his life, he had been waiting and wishing for this day, only to find that everything he had imagined was wrong. What a waste of time. His father was a pathetic drunkard with no spine and no moral compass. Benjamin was selfish and self-absorbed, and George was suddenly ashamed that he had come from such a deplorable man. Surely the entire Doughty family couldn't be so pathetic?

And then he was crying for Mamie, not with fury but with despair. George wished fervently that she was there with him, lending him her strength and conviction. When the girl made up her mind about something, she was fearless. She'd have bolstered him up, strategized, and sent him back into battle, only to fight right along beside him. How was he ever going to live his life without her? George felt the panic growing in him as he contemplated an entire, dismal lifetime without Mamie. It wasn't Christian, but there was a black hatred in his heart for Benjamin Upshur Doughty. It took some doing to collect himself, sitting there under the hickories. When he was calm once again, he stood up, brushed himself off, and headed back to the Methodist parsonage. There would be no more tears.

Beatrice was hanging the laundry to dry on the line in the side yard of the parsonage. It just so happened that it gave her an excellent view of the dirt road into town. She had been half-heartedly hanging wet clothing for some time now, eyes cut to the dusty Bayside Road. She hadn't figured it out immediately upon meeting George, but after studying him for some time over supper the prior evening, the astute woman had begun to suspect. Something about his nose. When the boy had said that his business was with their newly named deacon, she had known. She might not have all the details, but she knew enough to guess the importance of George's business. She also knew Benjamin Doughty well enough to predict the outcome.

The Reverend's wife had never taken to Benjamin the way her husband and the rest of the congregation had. Beatrice's gut never failed to lead her in the right direction, and something about Benjamin had always made her uneasy. Oh, he acted the perfect father and husband, doted on his wife and children in fact, at least in public, but the intuitive woman suspected there was much more to Benjamin beneath that spit shined surface.

So she hung clothes and waited until she saw a man walking down the road towards the parsonage and church. His shoulders were rounded and slumped, his head down, as if he'd fold his body in on itself and disappear. She sighed, but then said a quick prayer of gratitude that God had sent George back to her where she could care for him, at least temporarily. He walked slowly, scuffing his feet in the dust as if it were too much effort to pick them up and put them down, until he finally drew near enough for her to call out.

"Hello there, George! I've got butterbeans and corn left over from dinner. Let me heat you up a bowl."

"Thank you, Mrs. Myers. That's mighty gracious of you," George managed, following her in the backdoor of the parsonage and washing his hands before sitting down at the table. She set the pot of beans on the old, cast iron Reliance cook stove to heat, and, while they were warming, poured George a cup of tepid milk. Discovering he was mighty parched, George drank it straight down, so Beatrice poured him another. When she set the beans down before George, she wiped her hands on her yellow calico apron and took the seat opposite to quietly watch him eat.

When he was on his second bowl, she asked, "How did your business go today?"

Looking down at his bowl of beans, spoon hovering, he said nothing for a minute. But Beatrice had been so kind and George was so tormented that, before he knew what he was doing, he had set the spoon down and looked up at her. The dam broke and the words began to cascade out until he had told Beatrice everything, beginning with Lizzie and Benjamin, and ending with George and Mamie. Throughout Beatrice said not a word, just sat with her elbows on the table, hands folded, listening intently. Even as George described the day's encounter with Benjamin, she had kept her face carefully blank.

When he was done, George's eyes were red rimmed, but no tears fell. Beatrice, for her part, looked outwardly understanding and composed, but on the inside a tempest was brewing. She had, for the first decade of her marriage to Frederick, prayed and prayed for God to bless them with a child. For someone to throw such a beautiful soul away with nary a qualm was infuriating to the woman. She looked across the table at George, a lifetime of maternal emotion bubbling up, and she knew something must be done.

"George, my dear, I'd like for you to join us tomorrow at our church's spring picnic."

"I don't know, Mrs. Myers. I think I'd best be makin' my way home," he said, his voice flat and emotionally exhausted.

"I just won't take no for an answer, George. The guest room is still made up, and, by the way, you're to call me Beatrice."

George thought of that bed, comforting and soft. "I guess I'd like to stay the night if that's all right, Miss Beatrice."

"You run on along upstairs then and take a little nap. I'll wake you for supper. I've got some baking to do for tomorrow, and Frederick's gone doing Heaven's knows, so it'll be a nice quiet afternoon." George didn't hesitate.

When she heard the door close on the guestroom, she sat back in her chair, arms crossed, and her smile turned to a scowl. The entire Doughty clan would be at the picnic tomorrow, and she couldn't wait to see the expression on Benjamin's face when he saw his illegitimate son at the side of the Reverend and Mrs. Myers. Of course, she'd have to tell Frederick so he could plan Sunday's sermon accordingly, a sermon that she was determined for both Benjamin and George to be present to hear. She thought back to a day last spring when she'd seen a mama cat, fur standing straight off her body, run off a fox that had been after a kitten. That cat was fierce and dangerous, and so was the scowl on Beatrice's face.

Chapter Eleven

George's stomach woke him, gnawing at itself and growling like an angry dog. He had slept through supper the night before and, in that cloud-like bed, hadn't stirred until now. Although he didn't know it, Beatrice had peeked in on him around suppertime, saw him sleeping, and decided not to wake the young man. She pulled the thick quilt up to tuck him in tight, and simply gazed at the lad a few moments before tiptoeing out.

George threw on his clothes and splashed his face with water, hurrying downstairs to apologize to the Myers for sleeping through supper. Beatrice was making pancakes on the stove's griddle, and she turned to beam at George when she heard him come in. The Reverend however wasn't his usual jovial self, but sat frowning at his plate of pancakes.

Timidly, George offered, "Mornin' Miss Beatrice, Reverend."

"Good morning, dear. I hope you slept well," chirped Beatrice.

"Good morning, lad," grumbled Frederick.

Well, he guessed the Reverend knew. Beatrice must have shared his dreadful story. Thinking to save them any discomfort at having to ask him to leave, he resolutely said, "Thank you both for your kindness and hospitality. I'll be on my way."

Beatrice looked around at him, obviously distressed, and opened her mouth to speak, but the Reverend beat her to it. "Nonsense, lad! Sit your arse down here and help me with this pile of pancakes. I'll never get through the damned things myself."

George hadn't realized how stiffly he was holding his body until the relief coursed through him, and although he was sure the Reverend could handle that stack of pancakes, he nonetheless sat himself down to breakfast. Beatrice, smiling happily, shoveled more flapjacks onto the table, and all was quiet as the two men ate.

When the last pancake was gone, Beatrice cleared their plates and queried, "George, can I ask you to help me set up for the picnic? Those tables are awful heavy, and I just don't think that Frederick and I can manage them on our own."

After all they had done for him, George wouldn't deny her. "Of course, Miss Beatrice. You just tell me what needs doin', and I'll see to it.' George didn't catch the look of satisfaction that passed between the two.

While Beatrice was tidying up the breakfast dishes, George went upstairs and made the bed the best he could before heading out to change Pete's cabbage poultice. He pumped fresh water and hauled it in for Beatrice, and then the two set out for the church where the Reverend was awaiting them. The three made fast work of setting up the tables and preparing for the congregation, but throughout it all, no smile ever touched the Reverend's face. George remained uneasy, worrying that the tale he'd shared with Beatrice was sitting poorly on Reverend Myers, but the clergyman had nothing to say to George on the matter.

Beatrice, on the other hand, seemed quite happy and content to have George at their sides. She hummed as they worked, repeatedly telling the lad what a blessing it was to have him there. As they were bringing over the food which she had prepared the day before, George quietly asked her if everything was all right with the Reverend.

"Oh yes, George. There's a problem with one of the parishioners that he's working out in his head. He's just not sure how to handle it, and it's got him in a tizzy."

Reassured, George said nothing else on the matter. He stayed by Beatrice's side, ready to do her bidding. Before too long, people started to arrive, one family at a time, and Beatrice was careful to introduce George to every single soul, telling them all what a wonderful gift it was to have the lad with them. She stuck to him like glue, and for that George was grateful. He'd only ever been to one church picnic, and that was for the briefest of moments, so the lad felt awkward and unsure of himself. He braced each time he met someone new, a deep, primal fear telling him that he would be rejected, but they all just smiled and welcomed him to their gathering.

George wasn't sure, but he sensed that Beatrice was on edge as well, and he wondered if it was because of him. She kept looking around, as if she were seeking out someone she couldn't find, but he was sure they had spoken to every parishioner present, especially the children who gravitated to the Reverend's wife. One of the little one's was constantly tugging on her skirt to get her attention, and George smiled to see the happiness this gave the woman. If she wasn't tending to one of the older children, she was toting around a baby, careless of the drool they left behind on her calico dress.

Then something in the air acutely changed. He felt electricity crackle from Beatrice, and, startled, he looked to see her staring at the road as several wagons full of folks approached. Gone was the welcoming smile, and instead of heading to usher in the newcomers, she stayed rooted to the spot. George turned to see that the Reverend Myer was suddenly at their sides as well, also looking towards the road, just as gruff as he had been all morning. The two Myers exchanged a glance, both looking resolute and determined.

A whole slew of folks piled out of those three wagons, but, with sinking dread, George saw only one face. He heard a fellow near them shout out, "The Doughty's are finally here!", and everyone rushed over to greet the group. Everyone but George and the Myers. An older, haughty woman led the Doughtys, the rest of the family falling in behind like soldiers, and she nodded to everyone that she passed as if she was royalty.

She made her way to the Reverend and his wife, and with chin up and parasol planted, said, "Reverend Myers, Mrs. Myers. Good day to you both."

"Good day, Mrs. Doughty. I'd like to introduce you to our guest, Benjamin Hickman," Beatrice said, a challenge in her voice.

Mary Doughty looked George up and down, and with slight disdain introduced her husband and three of her children, one of which was Benjamin Doughty. George was torn between fear and wonder. These strangers were his family, all standing next to the man who had summarily dismissed George yesterday, the man who held his fate in his drunkard hands.

When the introduction fell on Benjamin, the man's eyes were furiously pinned to George who just looked back with outward calm and poise. Benjamin gritted out, "Good day to you, young man. Pleasure to meet you." George simply nodded.

Beatrice drew Benjamin's glare when she spoke, "I have thanked God over and over for bringing this wonderful, young man into our lives. This good samaritan helped my Frederick when the wagon became mired down coming back from tending Mrs. Drummond. George is such a kind, God fearing lad, I am certain that he must have been raised by exceptional parents." George cringed at not only the words but the ice in Mrs. Myers' voice. Beatrice, however, never took her eyes from Benjamin.

Benjamin needed to reply for the sake of superficial politeness, and, more importantly, to maintain secrecy, so he said tightly, "Effusive praise."

Then the Reverend Myers chimed in, "Is that spirits I smell? My nose must be playing tricks on me. I know my deacon and the upright Doughty Family better than that." He chuckled mirthlessly, the smile never reaching his eyes.

Haughty John O. grunted, Benjamin turned red, and Mary simply glared at the clergyman before saying to George, "Pleasure to meet you," and moving on, the rest of the Doughtys trailing behind. As he passed, Benjamin shot George a look of warning.

When the entourage had moved out of earshot, George turned to Beatrice, "Was that my grandmother?"

"Unfortunately for you, yes. As well as your grandfather, your Aunt Maggie, and your Uncle Richard."

"Are they always like that?"

"Yes," Beatrice spoke through a clenched jaw.

The Reverend Myer shook his head, sighing, obviously in a quandary. His inner convictions could not tolerate the sinful ways of this man who was one of his church elders, but he'd have to battle Mary Doughty to right the wrong, and, since she ruled Franktown, that meant risking the estrangement of his entire congregation. He felt like Daniel in the lion's den. Beatrice, sensing Frederick's inner turmoil, placed her hand on his shoulder, squeezing slightly, and George instantly thought of Mamie. How alike the two women were, loving, strong, and fearless, and his already high regard for Beatrice atmospherically soared.

The two Myers stayed with George, one of them always at his side as if on guard. Just like Honor, George smiled to himself, and the prior fear was replaced with gratitude and love. It wasn't long before the Doughtys said their goodbyes, only stopping briefly to give an empty thanks to the Reverend and his wife, who gave them a hollow reply in return. The Doughtys ignored George completely, even Benjamin. This seemed to be the signal to the rest of the congregation to say their farewells, and the families started trickling home.

When the last group had departed, Beatrice heaved a sigh of relief, and the three, weary people remaining set about cleaning up. George, still feeling the weight of his gratitude to the Myers, said, "Miss Beatrice, Reverend, y'all go on home and I'll clean this up."

"Bless your heart, son," the Reverend Myers proclaimed, "I'm tired as hell," and the two gathered some leftovers before heading back to the parsonage.

George made short work of taking down the tables and collecting the refuse, all the while replaying the afternoon in his mind. He thought with wonder at Beatrice and Frederick Myers who dispensed their love and care on George freely. So this must be what it felt like to have parents. Then he considered Lemuel and Old Whit, Mr. Scarborough and Doc Littleton, even the widow Bloxom. If he didn't need the recognition of his father so badly, he'd forget about the Doughty family and be grateful for those already in his life.

When the churchyard was returned to its former state of neatness, George went to visit Pete and see to his needs. He hauled more water for Beatrice, although she didn't need it, and then set about fixing the door on the little barn. The lower hinge had worked itself loose, and he had to dig around for some nails to fix it. By then the sun was getting low, and George went in to get cleaned up. The three of them sat around the table eating leftovers and laughing for hours before George, apologizing, excused himself for bed. He'd need a good night's sleep so he could set off for home bright and early tomorrow. As he sank into that blissful bed, no worries kept him awake, and he slept a dreamless sleep.

Downstairs, however, Beatrice and Frederick were at the kitchen table until much later, going over tomorrow's sermon and plotting their strategy. There was much debate on how to handle the situation with the Reverend leaning towards subtlety, his wife towards assertive outspokenness. He looked lovingly across the table at the woman who was ready to go in, guns blazing, for this young man who had so recently come into their lives. Not that he didn't feel protective too. He just preferred a less direct, combative approach. When they had the sermon nailed down, the two crept lightly up the stairs to bed. Neither slept as soundly as George.

Chapter Twelve

Sunday, May 15, 1882

When George awoke, he remembered that this would be the last time he rose from this wonderful bed so he took a moment to just lie there, reveling in the decadent luxury. Today, he would be headed home to that straw pallet by the cold hearth, but he'd always have the memory of the Myers and their hospitality. He was no longer certain how he felt about that buffalo skin, but he'd keep it, not just out of necessity, but as a reminder of what he'd learned about Benjamin Doughty, and also himself.

When he got downstairs, Beatrice was bustling about, a little flustered. "George, since it's Sunday morning, I've only got biscuits and jam for our breakfast. We'll need to be heading over to the church before too long."

"Well, Miss Beatrice, I'll just take mine with me. I'll see to Pete's fetlock before I go though."

"Go? Go where?"

"Why, I'll be headin' home, Miss Beatrice."

Just then, the Reverend waddled into the kitchen, dressed in his black suit, saying, "George, I was so hoping you'd join us this morning. I've prepared a damned, special sermon, and I'd be honored if you'd stay to hear it."

Looking relieved at her husband's intervention, Beatrice nodded eagerly. "Yes, George, do join us for Sunday service."

He was torn. He really needed to get on the road. He'd be late getting home as it was, but the couple had been so kind that he had a difficult time saying no.

"Yes, ma'am,' he sighed, "but I'll be needin' to leave right after."

Shortly thereafter, the trio headed over to the Franktown Methodist Church where Beatrice planted George at the end of the front row next to the piano where she took a seat and started playing. He wanted to hide in a corner in the back, but it would be rude to Miss Beatrice, so he just sat there trying not to fidget. He'd never been inside during a church service and sent a prayer to Heaven that he wouldn't act foolish and embarrass himself. He could hear folks coming in the church door, but it took him a good bit to work up the courage to turn around and look. Several people waved hello, and he nodded back in greeting, quickly turning back around to stare at the cross hanging over the pulpit.

George sat alone in the foremost row until he heard an imperious voice proclaim, "I believe we'll sit in the front today." Then a line of Doughtys were filing onto the bench, his grandmother, Mary, seating herself right next to George. Fire flashed in Beatrice Myers' eyes but her fingers never stumbled over the piano keys as she flawlessly played "Near the Cross". Everyone settled in, and George held himself ramrod straight, elbows close to his body, to prevent himself from inadvertently touching the arrogant woman.

Frederick H. Myer stepped up to the pulpit and said a prayer of invocation after which the congregation sang for a while. Then he started his sermon.

"Today, my flock, I will speak to you of Joseph, earthly father of Jesus. We are all familiar with the story of Jesus and the virgin birth, but I think we need to consider it from another perspective, that of the man who would raise Jesus as his son. You see, Joseph was betrothed to young Mary when he learned that she was to give birth to the son of God. Now, who amongst us, in the position of Joseph, wouldn't question Mary's honesty? Who wouldn't think that she had lain with another man, and, in so thinking, cast her aside? I have tried to imagine myself in similar circumstances and doubt that I would have the fortitude to bear up as well as Joseph.You see, he knew that should he not wed the girl, that she and the child would be shunned by society, cast out by her family, and left impoverished. Well, Joseph just happened to be an exceptional man for he could not abandon the girl and her unborn babe, leaving them to destitution. Leaving them to the community's hatred. Leaving them to a lonely life, being rejected by all." As he spoke, the Reverend's voice was getting louder and louder.

Suddenly, Reverend Myer slammed his fist down on the pulpit, "Joseph chose to protect the girl, to protect the child, all the while knowing that this would lead to great difficulties for himself!"

Then his voice softened as he continued, "I'd guess he was frightened by what his parents might think. I'd guess he was worried about how the community might treat him. I'd guess Joseph was concerned that the plans for his life would be disrupted by this unforeseen occurrence. But he chose the righteous path. God never said that it would be easy to walk in faith and live a Godly life, but Joseph trusted in God to see the three of them through this predicament. And so God did. What if he had made the easier choice? We will never know how God might have responded, but surely Joseph would have felt the Lord's disappointment every day of his life thereafter. "

The Reverend looked up at the parishioners glancing around the benches until his eyes locked on Benjamin Doughy who sat white as a sheet between his father and wife. "God calls on us all to make hard choices, but he promises to stand with us after, for all the days of our lives. He promises that if we trust in him, that he will hold us in the palm of his hand. I call on you all to make the hard but righteous choice."

His eyes never left Benjamin's ashen face as he said, "Let us bow our heads in prayer."

George knew now why the Myers had been intent on his staying for Sunday service, and his heart was full to bursting with love for the Reverend and his kind wife. He thanked God for putting Frederick Myers in his path and promised to always make the hard decision, the righteous decision. He thought of Reverend Kellam and how he preached fire and brimstone, especially in regards to Lizzie and George. He couldn't reconcile the two with their opposing messages but wished fervently that Pungoteague had a shepherd such as the Reverend Myers, a man who saw George not as a sin but as a Godly soul.

George remained seated on the bench until all the parishioners, Doughtys especially, had filed from the church, each stopping to greet the Reverend Myers and his wife at the door. He was only slightly curious how Benjamin had reacted to the clergyman, but he no longer had much concern for his father. Benjamin Doughty had only one thing of value to offer George, and that was his public acknowledgement. George wanted and needed nothing else from the pitiful man.

The preacher came back a few minutes later and sat on the bench next to George in the empty church. "I'm glad you stayed, son. It was important to me that you heard that sermon."

Choked up, George cleared his throat before saying, "You've given me a gift today that is more priceless than diamonds."

The older man nodded solemnly, "That's why I needed you to stay. To hear that the path Benjamin took was not the path of God. That is not what the Lord wanted for you or for your mother."

"Thank you sir."

"Now, George, I have put the idea in his head. Why don't you give Benjamin one last chance? Do you have the fortitude to make the hard decision?"

George looked up and slowly nodded. The two men stood and walked out of the church. Beatrice was waiting in the churchyard, wringing her hands. When Frederick saw her, he smiled, and she let out a breath.

"George, when you are finished with your business, I want you to come back by the parsonage so I can give you some provisions for the road, you hear?"

George wanted to embrace Beatrice, but he wasn't sure if that was acceptable, so he said simply, "Yes, ma'am."

"Off with you then," she shooed with tears in her eyes, and George set off for Franktown.

Mary and John O. Doughty were seated on his settee, Jane in a wingback chair, all three with unhappy looks upon their faces, and it seemed to Benjamin that all the chickens had suddenly come home to roost. He had no sooner returned from church, taken off his coat, and hung up his hat then there was a stern knock at the door. Jane had gone to answer, knowing of course who to expect, and had ushered in his parents who sat without being asked. Benjamin didn't try to appear cordial. That time had passed. His mother hadn't spoken a word to him since yesterday when that insipid, little preacher had coyly mentioned the smell of alcohol.

After that farce of a sermon today, he had intended to come home, lock himself in his study with a bottle, and spend the day feeling sorry for himself, so it was with great impatience that he said, "Let's get this over with."

Jane gasped at his belligerence, John O. grunted, but Mary Doughty didn't flinch. "Finally found your spine, have you, Benjamin?" she said casually.

Benjamin sat down across from the settee in a mahogany armchair and crossed his legs. "I've had a trying week, and I have no desire to spend my afternoon sparring with you, Mother."

It was clear to Benjamin that both John O. and Jane were there for appearances only, his mother's foot soldiers to be ordered about, and neither seemed inclined to join the fray. Just as well. He'd have his hands full with Mary as it was.

"I'm sure you can guess why we are here, Benjamin. After hearing from Jane how you've spent the past week, and then your father sharing your conversation of two days past, I felt the need to converse with you myself." Mary paused, waiting for Benjamin to speak up, but when he said nothing, she continued, "I am most unhappy with your behavior, but I find myself quite livid that the Reverend Myers would mention it at our church social. Can you explain to me how it is that he has been made aware of your sinful conduct?"

"I'm sure I couldn't say."

"I see. I don't suppose it has occurred to you that he would revoke your deaconship?"

Benjamin snorted. "That's what this is really about. You, Mother, are only concerned with how this will affect you. Queen Mary doesn't want her title tarnished. Don't pretend concern for me."

For a second, Mary's poise seemed to slip, but she regained her aplomb and continued, "I am concerned for all of us. Jane is quite embarrassed by your behavior. The way you spoke to your father was intolerable, and for it to be public knowledge is unacceptable."

"Do you wonder, Mother, why I drink?"

Mary considered him briefly before replying, "No. You've always been weak since you were small. It doesn't surprise me that you would handle yourself in such a way."

And there it was.

Just as Benjamin was about to stand and launch into a tirade that had been building for decades, there was another knock at the door. He bit back a roar of frustration and anger. Jane rose quickly, eager to escape the tension however briefly, and went to deal with the visitor. Not long after, she returned, looking quizzical, with George Hickman in tow. Benjamin no longer needed to scream, he wanted to cry, to lay down on his bed and sob himself into an exhausted sleep. It was too much to bear.

George didn't know what he had walked into, but the room was alive with tension. He hadn't expected his grandmother or grandfather to be present, and that gave him pause, but in for a penny, in for a pound. Perhaps they would swing the pendulum in his favor once George made them aware of the circumstances. There was nowhere to sit, and no one had offered anyhow, so he simply stood facing the room, hat in hand.

Jane apologetically said to Mary, "This is George Hickman. He said his business with Benjamin was urgent."

"We've met," the older woman dryly replied.

"Sorry for bargin' in like this, but I'm fixin' to head back home this afternoon, and I had to have a word with Benjamin first."

Mary Doughty regally swung her arm wide, inviting George to continue, but Benjamin leaped up from the armchair. "Why don't you and I go into the study, George."

"Don't be ridiculous, Benjamin," his mother said. "I'm sure it's nothing we can't hear."

"No, no," Benjamin was obviously in a panic. "We'll just be a moment."

"Sit down!" his mother ordered, and Benjamin did. Turning to George, "Please continue young man."

George took a deep breath, and began, "Benjamin is my father."

Again Jane gasped, John O. grunted, but Mary Doughty just chuckled. "I know."

Benjamin looked at his mother in astonishment, unable to speak, mouth agape, so the woman continued, "I've always known."

George looked between his father and grandmother, unsure of the family dynamics at play, but making a decision, he focused on Mary. "I've come to be publicly acknowledged by the Doughty family."

"I always knew that this day would come. I've been waiting for it, George," his grandmother placidly said.

A glimmer of hope started to flicker, a tiny spark in his heart, but the old woman quickly doused that flame when she continued, "You've come a long way on this fool's errand, young man. "

"I have come a long way, something I wouldn't of done if there was another way. I need Benjamin's acknowledgement to wed."

Mary huffed, "I know of no such law requiring a bastard to be acknowledged in order to wed."

"In Pungoteague, the word of Reverend Kellam is law."

Mary cocked her head quizzically, "So, you must be trying to marry someone above your station, boy. Otherwise, I can't believe the Reverend would much care."

"Pretty much everyone is above my station, thanks to your son. And the Reverend Kellam has made sure to remind me and every person in Accomack County of that fact since the day we met."

Benjamin could restrain himself no longer. "You think that me acknowledging you is going to change anything, you fool? You'll still be a penniless bastard. That public acknowledgement will, however, affect me, but I'm sure you couldn't care less about that."

George shook his head in disgust, and bit back the angry words ready to pour forth. That wouldn't help matters, might only hurt them. He knew he'd gain no ground with Benjamin, so he looked back to his grandmother when he pled, "I promise that if you grant me this, you will never lay eyes on me again. I am begging you."

The coldness in Mary Doughty's eyes told George all he needed to know. He had failed. He had lost Mamie, and his soul withered. Mary nodded to John O. who reached into the breast pocket of his coat and pulled out a thick leather wallet which he tossed to George who reflexively caught it.

"That," Mary sneered, "should be more than enough to buy you leaving this town in silence. That's a fortune for a man like you."

George stood looking down at the money in disbelief. A man like him. They thought to buy him off. "I don't want your money. There's only one thing I want from you, and it's not charity."

"This isn't charity, boy. This is a business transaction, and I consider it a wise investment," Mary retorted. "Take the money, and see yourself out."

George made a move to set the wallet down on a table, but Mary calmly stated, "If you don't take the money, I will call the law and say that you've been harassing us."

And George didn't doubt it. The young man, weary and defeated, looked to Benjamin. "All my life I've been longing' for you, and when I wasn't longing for you, I was wonderin'. What is my father like? Am I like him? Does he wonder about me? Your absence has been a hole in my pitiful, little life. I never wanted a penny from you, just a little of your time, and maybe your love. I wanted to know you, to learn from you, to look up to you. I wanted to feel like I had one person on my side. So, I didn't get what I came for, but I got somethin' else just as valuable. I got my freedom from you. I'm glad I met you all. I'll never wish to be part of this family again."

And with that, money in one hand, hat in the other, George walked out of the Doughty's lives forever.

As George headed south out of town towards the parsonage, he felt only numbness. He thought of all he should be feeling, but couldn't seem to conjure up any emotion. No doubt that would change with time, but for now, he just wanted to see Beatrice and Frederick Myers one last time, to thank them for all they had done for him. They would be so disappointed, and

George dreaded telling them his dismal news. He knew Beatrice, in particular, would suffer because of this, and he briefly thought about leaving town without telling the kind woman, but that was the coward's way out.

When he reached the parsonage, they were waiting, a bundle of food tied up in a cloth for the journey. Neither asked the outcome of the meeting because George's face told the story. When Beatrice embraced George, the first hug he had ever received, George held on tight and so did she. The Reverend Myers grasped his hand too tightly, not wanting to let go, and in the distance he heard Pete knickering from the barn.

"This has been the happiest time in my life. I wish with all my heart I could stay here and be part of your family. I've never known what it felt like to be loved by a mother and a father, but I'm thinkin' now I can guess. I have to go home, but it sure is gonna be hard to walk to that road. I am thankful for you, and you will have my love forever."

Beatrice was crying unabashedly and Frederick was swallowing hard. Beatrice managed, "I will remember you all the days of my life." George slowly walked to the road, but wouldn't let himself look back. He knew that if he did, he would stay, so he put one foot in front of the other, focusing only on that, until he was out of sight of the parsonage. Then a single tear rolled down his cheek.

Chapter 13

When George had come to the crossroads in Franktown last night, he had to make a decision: go east to Nassawaddox and try to hitch a ride north, or head north on the Bayside road and simply walk home. He didn't feel much like talking to anyone, so he just kept walking. The time and solitude to think seemed his best bet. He was grieving for Beatrice and the Reverend, and in absolute despair about Mamie. Lem had asked him what he had to lose by making this trip, and at the time the old man had seemed right, but now George was facing another reality. He had lost the dream of a father who was good and loving, and the hope of a steadfast, fearless wife and the children they would create together.

As he plodded along, he imagined telling Lizzie that her dream was lost too. His mother's soul was already fractured, and he worried that when he appeared without Benjamin, she would lose her last tenuous grip on reality. And Lem would be so disappointed. It would hurt telling his old friend that the last hope was gone. Mamie would go on and marry Josiah, and he hoped that she'd be happy, but he'd still have Honor. He sure looked forward to seeing his dog.

The Bayside Road wended and wheeled it's way up the west side of the peninsula, and, following the dusty track, George just managed to reach Nassawaddox Creek by the time the sun had set. He saw a small fire up ahead near the south bank of the creek, and as he drew near, could make out a man, smoking a pipe and gazing into the flames.

Not wanting to startle the man, he called out a greeting, "Hello, there!"

With no worry at all, the man waved, returning, "Howdy, stranger. What you doin' out here this time of night?"

George neared the campfire, seeing the man had a camp roll and a knapsack. "I'm heading north to Accomack. Name's George Hickman."

"Jeremiah Wilkins, but folks call me Jem. Have a sit down, if you're inclined."

George was, so he sat, eyeing the rabbit roasting on a spit. He took in Jem Wilkins and realized that the man was the same age as George, maybe even younger. Curiosity got the best of him, and George forwardly asked, "How is it you come to be out here on the bank of Nassawadox Creek sleepin' rough?"

Taking his pipe out of his mouth, Jem grinned, "I'm headin' to Dakota Territory. Gonna catch the PRR in Pocomoke and head up to Philadelphia. From there, I'll just hop one headed west."

"The PRR?"

"Pennsylvania Railroad. That'll take me all the way to Illinois. From there it'll be a far piece to pick up the Northern Pacific and head west to Dakota Territory, but if I make it that far, I can claim 160 acres."

"They just gonna give you 160 acres?" This seemed too good to be true.

Pulling the rabbit off the fire and taking out his knife, Jem began to make their dinner. As he carved, he said, "Yessir. Homestead Act of 1862. Now that they've got them Sioux under control, it's safe to farm, and there's a high call for wheat. *And* there's gold in the Black Hills."

George nodded thoughtfully, then asked, "Where you comin' from?"

"Down Wellington Neck. I'm the youngest of eight boys, and there ain't much for me here."

Jem handed George a haunch of rabbit, George thanked him, and, suddenly hungry, set to eating the greasy meat. When the rabbit was gone, George untied the cloth with Beatrice's parting gift and shared the apple pie he found.

"Well that's a fair trade," Jem chuckled.

"This gold," George ventured, "is just there for the takin'"

"Well, no claims to be had in Deadwood no more, but a bunch of fellas found a vein near Lead, called it Homestake. They's sendin' it up to Cheyenne by the coach full, if'in they can get by the road agents. Reckon' there's lots more gold to be found."

"You sure know a lot about gold minin'."

"Brother Zeke is out in Deadwood. Ever so often, we get a letter from him." George nodded thoughtfully.

Laying back beside the fire with his coat as a blanket, George listened to Jem ramble on about the glories of Dakota Territory and the riches to be had. Growing drowsy, George shut his eyes and imagined himself headed west. If it weren't for Lizzie, he had a mind to strike out himself. Him and Honor. He fell asleep thinking about gold in those Black Hills.

Monday morning George awoke before the sun, and, although grateful for Jem's hospitality, decided to get started alone. The other man was snoring soundly in his bedroll, and George wondered how Jem would ever get to Dakota Territory with so little gumption. He left half a loaf of bread and two apples as a thank you, pulled on his boots, shrugged on his coat, and started walking. As he plodded along, he almost immediately started in feeling sorry for himself. He sure had been dealt a bad hand. None of this was his doin', and it was all so unfair.

Again, he asked God why? But then he angrily thought that maybe God didn't care about a penniless bastard after all and didn't wait for an answer. Maybe Reverend Kellam was right all this time, and he was a sin in the eyes of the Lord. If that was the case, then God had seen to it that Mamie wouldn't be saddled with destitution and shame for the remainder of her young life. This was the path that the Lord had chosen for him, and he had no choice but to walk it, no matter how miserable and lonely that path was. That thought didn't sit too well, him having been so dutiful to God all these years, and he questioned the faith that he had put in his creator to guide and protect him.

"Ain't nobody gonna do that but me," he muttered to himself and the butterfly that fluttered by. He failed to notice the beautiful blue and black miracle as it lit on a wildflower by the side of the road.

Just after lunchtime, he passed the community of Craddockville, a cluster of ragtag shanties with disheveled children playing in the dirt outside. They all just stopped to stare, faces bereft of emotion, as he passed, and he wondered what they were thinking. No one responded to George's wave, and a scrawny woman appeared in a doorway to watch him walk on past. Her face also blank, she met George's gaze straight on, but ignored his halfhearted wave of greeting. He turned his gaze back to the road and picked up the pace.

About a half mile out of Craddockville, the skies opened up. George looked up into the deluge and wondered if this was God's answer to his earlier questions. So be it. He sprinted to the trees off the side of the road, looking for shelter of any kind. Nothing. He ran farther into the woods, tearing his shirt down the side on a limb. A short distance ahead, he saw an abandoned shack sitting alone in a copse of loblolly pines. Yes, he'd take care of himself. God was for those more fortunate.

Head down, he made a beeline for the door, and, throwing it open, tumbled in. He slammed the door, shook the water off, and looked up to see five shocked faces staring back at him. A black woman and four children of varying sizes sat at the table.

"Oh dear God! I am so sorry! I thought this shack was abandoned," he blurted out, appalled at what he had done. Then realizing his blunder, "I mean, I didn't see any smoke, so I thought no one was livin' here."

The woman calmly said, "Won't you come in, mister? It's comin' down hard out there."

George had his hand on the door, saying, "No, no, thank you, I'll be on my way. Please forgive me."

The woman gracefully stood. "I insist."

Hesitantly, George took his hand off the door and removed his battered hat. "I don't wanna intrude."

"The Lord has put you in our path, and I trust his judgment."

George could not currently say the same, but nodded his head. "I'm grateful, ma'am. I'll just sit quietly til the rain stops, and then I'll be goin'."

The woman nodded her head at a young boy who immediately leapt out of his chair. "Please have a seat. My name is Sary Randolph."

"George Hickman, ma'am. I'm much obliged."

With obvious pride, Sary pointed around the room at the children, saying, "These are my girls, Mary, Hanna, and Peg, and my oldest boy, Joseph." Looking back at the bed, with no less pride she said, "And this is my baby, Abraham."

Abraham was lying in bed propped up with pillows and wrapped in an old quilt made of scraps of clothing. The smile, although weak, was happy and true, until it was interrupted by a deep, rattling cough that shook the bed. Sary's smile faded for an instant, but then she turned it back on just as bright as she went to her boy. She fluffed his pillows, propped him up, and tucked the quilt around him before kissing his forehead and beaming at the lad who smiled sweetly back.

"Can I start a fire for you, Mrs. Randolph?" George asked, wanting to be of help.

"No thank you, Mister Hickman, we're savin' that wood for dark when it gets cold," Sary said with dignity. George looked at the meager pile of wood, dismally realizing that was all the Randolphs had. Because he couldn't rightly chop wood in the downpour, he just nodded.

"Will Mr. Randolph be along soon?" George asked, concerned that the man may not be happy to find a stranger in his home.

Although Sary said nothing, Joseph proclaimed, chin up, shoulders back, and chest out, "I'm the man of the house."

"That's right, sweetheart," his mama replied.

Again George just nodded, not knowing how to respond.

Sary eyed George's shirt, noticing the rent, and asked, "May I mend that for you, Mister Hickman?"

"Please, Mrs. Randolph, just call me George," he said, "and don't bother yourself with my shirt. I've already been trouble enough." Another cough came from the bed in the corner.

"Alright, George, but it's no trouble. We were just going to take turns telling Bible stories while we wait out this rain. Not much trouble to sew and listen." She lit the stub of a candle and got her sewing kit from under the bed.

The tallest girl, Mary, piped up, "Mama sews to make us money. She's real good at it."

"Very good at it, Mary," Sary corrected.

"Yes, ma'am."

Sary gestured for George to remove his shirt, and he obediently did so, afraid to defy her request. Hannah brought him a blanket which he wrapped around his nakedness like a cape while Sary laid his shirt on the table while she threaded her needle, and, looking at her eldest son, said, "Joseph, I believe that you will start. I'd like to hear the story of Simon Peter please."

Joseph, puffed up with importance at having George in the audience, moved to stand at the head of the table as if at a dais, and George guessed these recitations must be a regular occurrence. All the children sat attentively, and even little Abraham had his eyes glued on Joseph.

Joseph began, "The Apostle Peter's name was Simon before Jesus renamed him, and he was a fisherman, but when Jesus called Peter to join him, he dropped all that and became a 'fisher of men'." The child looked to his mother for approval, and Sary nodded encouragingly so he continued, "Peter was the first to call Jesus the Messiah, and he witnessed many of his miracles, like Jesus walking on water. He promised to be faithful to Jesus, but when the Romans came for Jesus and things got rough, Peter denied him not once, but three times! And Jesus was crucified, but God and Jesus forgave Peter for being unfaithful, so Peter spent the next thirty years as the leader of the apostles spreading the word of God."

Sary smiled at Joseph, saying, "Very good. Now tell me what we should learn from Peter, please."

Joseph paused for a moment, collecting his thoughts, then proudly said, "We should trust in God, and never deny him or Jesus."

"And?"

"If we mess up, God will forgive us."

Sary and all the children, including little Abraham, clapped their hands. Joseph grinned widely. The stories continued until each child had shared, even Abraham who spoke from the bed sharing the gory tale of Sodom and Gomorrah with obvious relish. His story was interrupted with coughing, but he determinedly got through and was lavished with praise from all the Randolphs. Outside the rain still pummeled the roof of the shack.

Sary looked up at George expectantly, biting off the thread as she finished mending his shirt. "Would you care to take a turn, George?"

Caught off guard, he stammered out, "Um..Um..Yes. I mean, yes ma'am," and rose to stand at the head of the table. He shared the story of the prodigal son who was lost but then found, and the Randolph family listened approvingly.

"His father forgave him, and accepted him lovingly back into the family," George finished.

"And what is the message, George?" Sary prompted.

"That we oughta try to forgive like God, who will open his arms to us all, if we just ask for mercy."

"I forgave Mary just yesterday for pulling my hair," Hanna added.

"And I forgave you for calling me an idgit which is why I pulled your hair," Mary retorted.

With the two girls glaring at each other, Sary calmly looked between them and said, "You know better than this, especially in front of company," and Mary and Hanna looked down contritely at their laps.

Sary stood, shaking out George's shirt, and showed the mended tear to the man, who couldn't help but admire her handiwork. "Mighty fine work, Mrs. Randolph." He turned his back to don the shirt, and turning back, neatly folded the blanket.

"Thank you, George." Outside the rain still beat down rhythmically. "I guess it's just about supper time."

As if on cue, the girls jumped up and went over to the stove and pulled out a half loaf of cold bread while Joseph took mismatched plates and cups down from a shelf to set the table. Dinner turned out to be slim pickins', and George opened up the towel of food Beatrice had sent. Inside were several slices of ham, four boiled eggs, and two apples. When George added his haul to the half loaf of bread and jar of apple butter, Sary tried to hide the relief in her eyes. She divided everything equally onto the plates, and going to the bed, gently picked up Abraham to sit him in her lap at the table.

The two shared a plate, and the frail boy ate sparingly, Sary encouraging him to take every bite. Paroxysms of coughing interrupted his feeble attempts to chew, and once a chunk of ham flew from his mouth onto the table. Everyone pretended not to notice, while Sary quickly cleaned it up. The other four children cleaned their plates to the last crumb which caused George to silently wonder about their lives. When they had all finished, Joseph cleared the table while the girls washed the dishes, and Sary tucked Abraham back into bed.

Since it was getting dark and the rain still hadn't let up, Sary decided that George would stay the night with the Randolph family. "You can sleep next to Joseph and share his blanket, George."

The family gathered around the table for their nightly prayer, and Sary began, "Thank you God for this day which I am blessed to have spent with all five of my children. Thank you for allowing us to do your work in helping George. Guide him in his quest, Lord." At this George turned his eyes up sharply, but Sary continued, "And watch over my baby, Abraham. Not a sparrow falls...We thank you God. Amen.

The children immediately dispersed, the girls pulling blankets out from under Abraham's bed. Joseph went to the old, iron stove and began to put the few sticks of firewood in to start a meager fire. In short time, the one room shack had gotten marginally warmer, and all five children were asleep. Sary and George still sat at the table.

When George began to stand, Sary bade him sit a while, so the young man did.

"Where are you from, George?"

"Cashville, west of Onancock, Mrs. Randolph."

"Where are you going?"

"Home from Franktown."

"Was your trip successful?" Sary oddly queried.

Surprised by her question, George only quietly said, "No."

The ebony skinned woman only nodded her head as if she already knew. George, feeling safe with Sary, added, "I'm a bastard. I went to Franktown to try to get my father to acknowledge me, but him and his family turned me out."

Sary only nodded sagely so George filled the silence by sharing his tale. The second time he'd spilled his guts to a near stranger, he thought. Strangely enough though, he felt that Sary was a haven for his confusion and possibly a source of wisdom.

When he was finished, Sary said, "God has a plan for you, George. I know your faith has faltered, but don't turn your back to him. He will see you through this."

He wasn't sure how she knew, having only met him hours before, but he accepted her words. "You're right, Mrs. Randolph. I've been weak the past few days."

"You don't need your father's acknowledgment, George. That isn't worth two cents and won't change a thing. You'll still be a bastard. And you will still be a good and worthy man."

George sat thinking about her words for a few long moments and realized she was right. He *had* been on a fool's errand, just like Mary Doughty had said. Although he might despair at the loss of his Mamie, he needed to accept that this was what God wanted for him. Time to be a man.

"Mrs. Randolph, you're right. Thank you for your wisdom."

She smiled at George, saying, "What you need, you already have. Believe in yourself, George, the way that God believes in you."

The two sat a few moments in silence before George quietly asked, "What ails Abraham?"

Sary stiffened a little, and George wondered if he'd overstepped his bounds but then realized that it simply hurt her to talk about the sick boy. "I'm sorry that I asked. You just pay no nevermind to me, Mrs. Randolph."

Sary just shook her head. "I suspect that God sent you to me for a reason, that being that I don't have anyone to talk to, just my children." And with that she commenced her tale.

Sary's husband, Henry Randolph, worked as a mate on a white man's fishing boat out of Craddockville, mostly crabbing and such. When the fisherman's wife had come up pregnant, not of the fisherman's doing, she had accused Henry of raping her. He had left one morning and never returned, a mob of folk waiting for him at the dock with the fisherman leading the call for justice. The folk of Craddockville had summarily hung Henry from the nearest tree, the fisherman's wife in attendance. The baby had come out white.

Without a tear in her eye, Sary spoke matter of factly, "That was two years past."

Horrified, George choked on his words. He had heard about lynchings but fortunately had never witnessed such an atrocity. Lem could tell stories, but they were from years past, and George had mistakenly thought that the new era of emancipation had ended that barbaric injustice. In George's dismayed silence, Sary continued her story.

A trained seamstress, the woman took in all the work she could find. The children helped by picking up and delivering her work and in their spare time tending their little garden. Joseph did some fishing which was a great boon, and Mary was almost old enough to go into service if necessary. Sary told her tale with little emotion, and George wondered at her poise and dignity. There was no self-pity in her voice, just a statement of fact, but still she had not answered his question about Abraham. Then George saw her face change, and it was painful to witness.

With obvious grief, Sary began talking about her youngest son. "Almost a year ago, Abraham developed a cough. I thought it would pass, but it only worsened." She took a deep breath before continuing to tell George that she had worked long into the nights to gather the extra money she needed to take Abraham to see the doctor in Belle Haven. The other children had willingly sacrificed meals and looked for odd jobs to hasten the process. When she finally had enough money to pay the doctor, his diagnosis had been consumption.

"That white man acted like Abraham caught that disease because he was a poor, dirty, black child. When I asked him what to do for Abraham, he said there was a new treatment available in Philadelphia. They would puncture my boy's chest to collapse his lung so it could heal, but it was useless to consider because I couldn't afford it." Her righteous anger was clear in her voice.

She continued. "Then that doctor told me to send Abraham to a sanatorium for poor folk in Baltimore. Can you believe that he wanted me to send my baby away to never see him again?" Gone was the dignity, even the anger, replaced by the anguish of a mother. "He said that we'd all get sick if Abraham stayed here, and that he was sure to die anyway." At this tears began rolling down her cheeks, and George had never felt so helpless. He reached across the table and took her hand, knowing it was improper but needing to express his empathy. Sary didn't pull her hand away.

"My baby is going to stay right here until God calls him home."

Sary's tears took a time to dry up, and when they finally did, she rose, saying, "Thank you for listening and for caring, George Hickman. Goodnight now." She went over and climbed into bed with Abraham, setting off a coughing spell. When the lad settled, she wrapped herself around the boy, and pulled the quilt tight around them. George laid down next to Joseph but, not wanting to disturb the sleeping child, didn't bother with the blanket and instead used his coat again for its nominal warmth. Sleep was a long time coming as he realized that his problems were maybe not that great after all.

Chapter 14

Wednesday, May 18, 1882

George was weary, but he was almost home, and he wanted to see his dog so he pushed on. He had been walking forever, or so it seemed, and he had a blister on his heel the size of a silver dollar. He hadn't eaten all day which added to his misery, but he felt spiritually less burdened than he had in weeks.

The day before had been spent with the Randolphs, or more definitively in the piney woods near their shack. He had chopped wood until his hands blistered, the blisters broke, and every swing of the blade was sheer agony. Thinking of Abraham, he worked through the pain and kept going until the light could no longer find its way through the loblolly branches and he could barely see the axe hit its target. He reckoned, with satisfaction, the Randolphs had half a cord of wood now, enough to keep the stove burning for a while. Joseph had gone fishing while George worked and had returned home triumphantly with two striped bass. Added to the loaf of bread Sary baked, George and the Randolph family enjoyed a meager but satisfying meal. He had bunked again with Joseph near the now well stoked fire, and slept soundly through the night on the rough, plank floor.

The dawn had awoken him, and hurriedly, having slept in his clothes, he slipped out of the shack without waking the woman and her children, but not before he had left the leather wallet filled with bills on the table. He wasn't sure how much was in the wallet and had never thought to count it, but he hoped it was enough to pay for that new treatment Sary had been talking about. If it wasn't, well then, it would certainly supply a goodly amount of food for the family. Either way, he was rid of the burden and felt lighter for it. George knew that Sary wouldn't accept the money willingly, so he put his boots on outside the shack and slipped away with no goodbye. He hoped his gift would be thank you enough for the kindness the family had shown him.

George wove his way through the trees, footsteps silent on the pine shats, all the while reflecting on his time with the courageous Randolphs. By the time he had come back out to the road, George knew a few things with absolute certainty. One, God had sent him to this family to show him humility. Sary Randolph didn't waste one second feeling sorry for herself, and her faith in the Lord never faltered. What that family had suffered caused George shame for the self pity he had allowed himself. The other thing George knew for sure was that he didn't need the acknowledgment of the Doughty family after all. Their name wouldn't change the first thing, not in George's character and certainly not in the direction his life would lead.

As he walked along the Bayside road towards Pungoteague, passing through Boston late that morning, the confused thoughts in George's head started to sort themselves out and a plan began to crystallize. He had come to accept the loss of Mamie, and while he still grieved for the girl, he knew that he'd been beat. The way he saw it, he had two choices. George could either wallow in his misery, or he could make the best of the hand he'd been dealt. He had let go of the hurt and disappointment the Doughty family had bequeathed him, leaving that behind in Craddockville thanks to Sary Randolph, and he walked with his head up and his shoulders back.

Although he hadn't quite attained the self esteem that Sary had encouraged, at least he was no longer ashamed of who he was.

And he had a plan. George was heading west, just like Jem Wilkins. He would sell the two acres and the chickens, give Lucky to Lem, and seek a better life where no one knew him or his past. Sure, it was a risk, but he had little to tie him to Pungoteague. Just Lizzie, the fly in the ointment. At first, he had dismissed the plan because of his responsibility to his fragile mother, but the more he walked, the more this chafed. He had finally decided he would give her a choice to come with him or stay on her own. Either way, he was leaving Accomack County behind.

Mamie had been in a turmoil for over a week, and she wasn't sure how much longer she could take this limbo while holding her emotions in check. George hadn't been at the north branch last Tuesday, no surprise after that weasel, Reverend Kellam, had humiliated the man. She desperately needed to speak with him, had to know where his head was and what he was intent on doing. All her plans hinged on him, and Mamie would be in purgatory until she could see George. She hadn't seen him in weeks, and George's absence left a void in her life. Her misery, added to the anger and fear, created a volatile emotional brew.

The whole town was abuzz with the gossip of George's visit to the Miller home, and Mamie had bitten her tongue until it bled rather than berate every loose tongued fool who was chattering about the best man that Accomack had ever produced. She had limited her response to a long, malignant glare, taking satisfaction when the townsfolk had scurried away in shame. Her mother had commented wryly, "If' you're not careful, your face'll freeze that way." Mamie had just huffed indignantly and continued glaring.

William Miller was fairing no better than his daughter. Caught between a rock and the Reverend Kellam, his life had become a living hell. Mamie had sat rigidly beside him on the buckboard the entire way to Onancock yesterday, and never uttered a single word despite his pitiful attempts at conversation. His wife, however, *was* speaking to him, albeit in aloof and polite monosyllables, but even his youngest son, Fitz, had taken the side of the women.

Truth be told, William didn't really dislike George Hickman. In fact, he admired the lad's gumption, but he had a higher law to answer to. Letting Mamie marry George would be a sin in the eye's of God, or so Kellam said, an edict the sailor had found himself beginning to question in the past days. What would really be so terrible about his daughter marrying the illegitimate boy? But this thought he wisely kept to himself.

Mamie had found it easy to rebuff her father's attempts at reconciliation. Her life was hanging in the balance after all, and the man seemed to care not one whit. She had only endured that long, silent, uncomfortable ride to Onancock yesterday because she wanted news of George, and she knew Louisa Guy, that silly goose, would have all the gossip. As soon as William had hawed the horses to a stop at the wharf, she'd gathered her skirts and leapt down, stomping off to the mercantile where Louisa was waiting, eager to share her news. Mamie had promptly learned that George had set out for Northampton County last week and nobody had seen him since. Louisa continued to prattle on about all that George had purchased while in town Monday last, up to and including the loaf of bread, but Mamie wasn't listening. She was wondering about Northampton County.

Feeling quite important, Louisa expounded on the details with only slight exaggeration, declaring, "He had extremely important business down there. The way he was dolled up, I'm quite sure he'd gone south to propose marriage."

Louisa had waited expectantly for a reaction from Mamie, hoping for histrionics, and was disappointed when Mamie said only, "I see."

"I'm so truly sorry, dear Mamie! I know you must be heartbroken to hear such sorrowful news. I wish I wasn't the one to deliver such a heavy blow to you, dear friend," Louisa poured it on thick, still desiring some melodrama to fuel the gossip mill.

Mamie snorted, "Still got your sights on Josiah? If you do, Louisa, you'd better hope George wasn't on such an errand. I'll gladly give you Josiah back once George returns." Louisa gasped, her hand over her mouth. Mamie stuck her tongue out at the girl and stomped back out of the mercantile.

When Mamie had returned to the wharf where her father was haggling with Seth Robbins, she saw a parcel in the back of the wagon, wrapped in brown paper and tied with string. Still infuriated over her exchange with Louisa, she gave little thought to the package until her father brought it up halfway home to Pungoteague.

"There's a bolt of blue calico back there that will match your eyes perfectly, Mamie." So he was going to try to bribe her, was he?

When she said nothing, he quietly added, "It's for your wedding day a week from Saturday. Your mama's gonna make you a new dress."

"So you're really gonna make me do this?" she said with tears already running down her cheeks.

"I got no choice, girl."

"There's always a choice."

As the Bayside Road brought George nearer and nearer to Pungoteague, he wrestled with the desire to stop and have one final word with Mamie. He realized sadly that she was now a loose string he had to tie up, and there were things he needed to say, but after his last visit to the Miller home, he questioned the wisdom of such a venture. Shrugging his shoulders for no one to see, he thought he could stand another tongue lashing if Mr. Miller was home. He would pass right by their home, and this might be the last chance he had to say goodbye.

As he stood on the stoop and knocked, heart in his throat, he wished his hound was there to lend his support, and George let out a sigh of relief when Mrs. Miller answered the door instead of Mamie's father.

The nervous, young man thought he saw her lips twitch slightly at the corners before she said, "George Hickman. I've been wondering where you've been."

Slightly confused by her response, he blurted, "Northampton County."

"So I heard."

"Mrs. Miller, please may I see Mamie? Just for a minute. It won't take long, but I gotta tell her somethin'."

"You're in luck, George. William is somewhere on the Chesapeake between here and Baltimore, so I guess Mamie can spare a moment. Won't you come in?"

Shocked by the invitation, George hesitated. "I don't think Mr. Miller would like that much."

"You let me worry about that, George," she said, stepping back out of the doorway, arm sweeping wide.

And there Mamie stood in the middle of the parlor in a partially completed blue calico dress, straight pins precariously stuck everywhere. Her hands on her hips, she stated irritably, "It's about time you got here."

"Hello, Mamie."

"Hello, George. I've missed you."

"Been down in Northampton County this week past."

Mamie snorted, an unladylike habit her mama just couldn't break, and said, "The whole county knows that. Louisa Guy tried to tell me you were down there proposin' to another girl, but I don't believe that."

"No, wasn't that t'all," and George told her the whole tale, start to finish, dwelling especially on the Myers and their kindness. When he was finished, she was quiet for a beat before she quietly said, "You never said, George. About Benjamin I mean."

"Never no need to, I guess. He wasn't important until your daddy said why I couldn't marry you. Then I got this hairbrained idea that if I could get Benjamin to just say publicly he was my father, that everythin' would magically change, the Reverend would suddenly accept me, and your daddy would let us marry. Silly, huh?"

Mamie had never been prouder of George. All this time she had been doubting his commitment to her, and he was getting his heart broken by a bunch of selfish, high and mighty fools. Why, she had a mind to go right down there to Franktown and tell those Doughtys what they could do with their name, but she had bigger fish to fry right here in Pungoteague.

Before she could answer, George commented, "That's a right pretty dress, Mamie. The blue matches your eyes exactly."

Looking down at the dress sadly, Mamie said, "It's my wedding dress."

George just nodded, a lump in his throat.

She continued, "A week from Saturday."

After an awkward pause, George cleared his throat and said, "I came to tell you goodbye, Mamie. I'm selling my stead and heading west, maybe to Dakota Territory. Just leaving Accomack, going where no one knows me and startin' over. I wanted to thank you before I went for bein' one of my few, true friends. I shouldn't say this now, but I love you, Mamie, and I want you to have a happy life, even if it ain't with me. You're a good woman, you'll make Josiah a fine wife."

Mamie was abruptly overwhelmed with the thought of never seeing George again. He might just as well be dead, the grief she felt. Yes, it was grief, bone deep, desperate, unbelieving grief. This just couldn't be. She couldn't imagine her entire life without him, and yet, she knew that if they couldn't marry, it would be selfish to ask him to stay, to see her with Josiah. So she simply nodded, unable to speak.

"I best get goin' before your daddy gets home. Take good care, Mamie." And he was gone.

Belatedly she said what she had been thinking all along, "I love you too, George."

When Mary Doughty returned, she found the dress in torn pieces on the floor.

This time when George left the Miller home to walk through Pungoteague, he did it with his head up, straight and tall. He was miserable at the loss of Mamie, but that chapter of his life was now done, and he was moving on. He nodded or waved to all the folk who called out their greetings as he passed, welcoming him home. But no, it wasn't his home. Still he carried himself with dignity, and Mr. Scarborough and Doc Littleton, debating later over the pot bellied stove in the mercantile, couldn't make heads or tails of it . He left the road after crossing Taylor Creek and made short work of the remaining miles to Cashtown.

George was within a mile of the shack on the old deer path through the woods, lost in thoughts of dread, sadness, and hope. Dread at facing his mother, despair over the loss of Mamie, and hope for what the future might bring. So engrossed in his mind's inner workings, he was paying scant attention to his surroundings. Coming around a bend, he was suddenly on his back struggling to breathe, a heavy beast standing on his chest. He quickly rolled to the side onto his hands and knees, shielding his head and catching his breath. When he could breath, he knelt and opened his arms to his dog, laughing and hugging him fiercely to his body. Honor cried in pitiful yelps, the likes of which George had never heard from his dog. He struggled to be free of George's embrace only to throw himself back into the man's arms, wagging his tail frenetically. When both the man and dog had exhausted themselves in greeting, they continued down the path towards the shanty, both overjoyed at their reunion.

Breaking through the trees into the clearing where the shack sat, George took it all in with a melancholy sigh. It wasn't going to be easy to give up something for which he'd worked so hard, but his mind was made up. The chickens were clucking contentedly as they scratched around the yard, and Lucky lifted his head up and brayed at the sight of his master home at last. He expected to see Lizzie step out onto the stoop with that feverish hope lighting her eyes, but no one stirred, just himself and the animals. It was only then that he noticed the two horses tied out with Lucky and the buckboard wagon partially hidden by the shack. He set a direct course for the door of the shack, but when he was only halfway across the clearing, his grandfather, Edward Hickman, stepped out of the door.

George stopped dead in his tracks, flummoxed at the sight of the man who he hadn't seen for nigh on fifteen years. Confused, he started slowly walking towards his grandfather, although Honor ran up to Edward as if they were the best of friends, something that confounded George even more.

The younger man stopped twenty feet away. "Edward. What's the meanin' of this?"

"Hello there, George. You've grown into a fine man."

George didn't have time for niceties, certainly not from a man who allowed him and his mother to be turned out in poverty. "Just get to it, Edward. Why are you here, and where's my mother?"

Edward had the decency to look shame faced. "She's not here, George."

"Where is she?" He was beginning to worry. He could count on one hand the number of times she had left the stead.

"It's a bit of a story, son."

"Well, you'd best get to tellin' it then."

Honor stood between them now, looking confused by the tension, wagging his tail uncertainly.

"The Reverend Kellam was here Wednesday past. The afternoon you left for Northampton." Suddenly, George's heart was in his throat as his grandfather told the tale.

The clergyman had shown up that afternoon, the gossip from Onancock having spread, as George had predicted, clear across Accomack County. Kellam had made the eight mile trip to inform George that his journey to Northampton County would be a wasted effort. Though he missed George by more than half a day, Lizzie was home, and never one to pass up an opportunity, the Reverend had bullied his way inside and laid waste to the tiny fragment of sanity Lizzie had remaining. She had fled the shanty in her nightclothes, running barefoot cross country to the only other place she knew to go.

When Lizzie reached her father's farm several miles away, her feet were bleeding, her hair was wild, and she was sobbing incoherently. Ann was in the process of turning her stepdaughter away, when Edward came out of the barn.

In a voice Ann had never heard, Edward proclaimed, "Enough!"

He walked straight at Lizzie, who, unsure, backed up a few steps, but he kept coming only to take her in his arms and hug her tightly to him. For several long minutes, she convulsively cried, Edward rocked her in his arms, and Ann stood by helplessly.

When she had calmed enough to speak, Edward asked, "What's happened, Lizzie? Is it George?'

Lizzie shook her head and said only, "Kellam."

Edward nodded knowingly, and, turning to Ann, ordered, "Get my daughter inside, get her cleaned up, and get her some clothing. I'll be in shortly."

Some time later, Edward had the whole story, all the sordid details, and was vacillating between shame and fury. Keeping his face carefully blank, he said, "Lizzie, you'll sleep in Rosie's bed tonight. I can take you home on the morrow, if you so wish."

Looking down at the table, Lizzie said, "Don't wanna go back there."

"Well, head on up to bed for now, and we'll talk more in the mornin'."

Like an automaton, she arose and did as she was told, leaving Ann and Edward to argue long into the night. Ironically, it was Ann who finally came up with a solution that would satisfy them both.

The next morning Edward hitched up the horses to the wagon, and Ann headed into Bobtown to see Eleanor Edmonds, a widowed woman with failing eyesight in desperate need of a live-in companion. The two mile trip was too brief for Ann who fretted the entire way about what words she'd use to convince Eleanor to take a chance on Lizzie. The entirety of Accomack County knew her stepdaughter's sordid story, and if Eleanor didn't accept her on then Ann would be saddled with the harlot, an unacceptable situation. Ann was banking on the drama of Lizzie's latest pickle to win Eleanor over, if only out of pity.

Stopping the wagon in front of the neatly whitewashed picket fence surrounding the tidy little home, Ann tied the horses up and let herself through the gate. Eleanor was already at the open door having heard the harness jingling some distance away.

"Good day, Eleanor. It's Ann Hickman."

"Well, hello there Ann. What a surprise." There was an undercurrent of censure in the woman's voice.

Ann suddenly felt a little out of her depth. "I've got a proposition for you, Eleanor. May I come in?"

The handsome woman stepped away from the door, somewhat reluctantly thought Ann, and she entered the Edmonds home. The inside was no less prim and proper than the out, and when Eleanor bade her sit, Ann perched nervously on the edge of a chair, careful to touch nothing.

Austerely, Eleanor queried Ann, "So what brings you, Ann?"

Used to bullying her way through life, it was with uncharacteristic timidity that Ann spoke. "My stepdaughter is in need of a position. It occurred to me that you might find her services useful in your current condition."

"So you think me incapable in my 'current condition'?"

Thrown, Ann stuttered, "No, no....not incapable. No not incapable. I simply thought that she could make life easier for you..."

Ann would have continued to ramble on if Eleanor hadn't abruptly interrupted, "So why does Lizzie need a position now? Where is George?"

So the sly old she-wolf knew all about her stepdaughter's vile history. Of course she did, as did everyone in Accomack County. This was going to be harder to sell than Ann had expected, especially to this crusty queen bee with her perfectly coiffed hair and lace trimmed gown.

"Elizabeth has gotten herself into another mess. Last evening she appeared at our home disheveled and distraught, ranting on about being assaulted by the Reverend Kellam. Now I know it's unlikely to be true..."

"Is it?"

Again Ann paused, taken aback by Eleanor's derisive tone. "Why, of course. I'm sure Elizabeth has, in her fragile state, misconstrued the Reverend's actions."

"So you'll not have her at your home even now?"

Ann was rendered dumb and sat in appalled silence until Eleanor, nonchalantly toying with the string of pearls around her neck, continued, "You're here because you're looking to foist Lizzie off on me, am I correct?" Ann was looking at the door and wondering how she could make an exit while retaining some modicum of dignity when Eleanor stated firmly, "Bring her to me. *She's* more than welcome here."

Ann, knowing what was implied, stood and took her leave. "Thank you, Eleanor, and good day." The woman only nodded in return leaving Ann to see herself out.

Ann returned to the farm looking for a victim to bully and demanded that Edward tell Lizzie of her new circumstances. Had she not already done the lion's share in securing the position? Besides, Lizzie was sure to stage a show, ungratefully refusing Ann's hard won victory, but yet again Ann Hickman was thrown off guard when Elizabeth quietly thanked her father in agreement, seemingly content with the arrangement. How like her to show no gratitude to Ann for all she had done.

The next morning at the breakfast table, Ann had held her breath as Edward had unexpectedly made clear to Lizzie that the choice to join Eleanor Edmonds was hers and hers alone. "You are welcome here. I will never turn you out again," the old farmer had said with suspiciously damp eyes.

Lizzie, looking at her plate, nodded. "Thank you father, but my presence here would cause unnecessary strife." Edward had looked hard at Ann who self-righteously lifted her chin high with haughtiness in response.

After breakfast, Edward had once again hitched the team to the wagon, helped Ann onto the buckboard bench and Lizzie into the back, and set out for Bobtown. Ann had tried mightily to remain behind, but Edward would have none of it.

"Woman, this is your doing, so make ready to go. I'll not hear one more word from you on the subject." The three had ridden in silence the entire way.

Again, Eleanor, looking almost regal in her muslin day dress, was standing in the open door, but this time she called out a greeting, "Hello Edward. Hello Lizzie," intentionally skipping over Ann.

"Good day, Mistress Edmonds," Edward called as he escorted Lizzie up the walk, Ann lagging behind.

"Lizzie, I'm Eleanor Edmonds, and I'm very pleased to make your acquaintance," the old hag warmly greeted Ann's stepdaughter.

Lizzie was clear eyed and focused when she replied, "Mistress Edmonds. Thank you for this opportunity."

"Lizzie, you've been through enough in this life. It's high time you landed somewhere safe." At this Ann rolled her eyes, but Edward looked down at the ground in shame. Eleanor reached out an arm to draw Lizzie to her and hugged her briefly, before setting the woman to her side and looking towards her father, saying, "You can visit on occasion," an invitation once again pointedly ignoring Ann.

"Thank you, Mistress Edmonds. You have our gratitude," the old farmer said contritely, and before he and Ann could turn to leave, Eleanor had ushered Lizzie, who went quite willingly, into her home and shut the door. The two stood staring at the closed door momentarily, then, with not a word, they were back in the wagon headed home.

When the buckboard had hawed to a stop in the Hickman farmyard, Edward made no move to get down. With a huff, Ann, gathering her skirts, got herself down, and looking up at Edward snapped, "Where are you off to?"

"Headed to Cashville."

His wife narrowed her eyes. "When you plannin' on bein' back?"

"When George don't need me no more."

She wanted to stomp her foot in fury, but turned on her heel and paraded into the house. She'd never be rid of those two leeches.

With not another thought for the harridan, Edward made tracks intent on minding George's stead until his return. The old man had been there since Friday last, almost six days ago, tending Lucky and the chickens, and keeping Honor company. Lemuel had shown on Saturday, and the two men had spent a considerable amount of time discussing a myriad of issues, all revolving around George. By the end of the day, a friendship had been struck, and the two felt that they were now working towards a common cause.

Lemuel's primary concern was George's reaction when he learned of what the Reverend Kellam had done to his mother. Underneath the lad's calm exterior ran a deep river of emotion. A river that might just overflow its banks should there be a storm. Lem figured this had been building for some time, and if he and Edward weren't careful, the boy could get himself in a world of hurt. Edward was embarrassed to admit that the old, black man knew his grandson better than he, so he simply deferred to Lem's judgment on the matter.

When his grandfather had finished the woeful tale, Edward still stood in the yard, dangerously still. He said not one word, but turned on his heels, and set off for the deerpath back towards Pungoteague. Before he could get more than a few feet, Edward urgently called, "Wait! Take a breath, boy. Stop and think a minute!"

Glaring, George turned and nailed his grandfather to the stoop with his eyes. "What is it I'm supposed to be thinkin' of? To turn the other cheek? To let God judge that monster? This time I ain't gonna stand by and let him get away with it!"

"Go see your mother first, boy. She's safe now. See for yourself. Give yourself a day for your blood to cool, then decide what your next step's gonna be."

Although he didn't want to admit it, needed an outlet right this minute for his fury, the old man was right. "Where's this Edmonds woman live?"

When Lizzie opened Eleanor Edmond's door an hour later, George was stunned into stupidity. There stood his mother with hair brushed and plaited, wearing a new calico dress, and almost smiling.

"Won't you come in, George."

The clearness of her green eyes dampened the fire he'd been stoking, if only a bit. Taking off his old, felt hat, he followed his mother into the bungalow's sitting room where Eleanor was sitting in a floral armchair, drinking chamomile tea from a china cup.

"Good day, Mrs. Edmonds."

"You must be George! Your mama has told me so much about you." George, looking to Lizzie, thought he must surely be dreaming.

"Yes, ma'am."

"Well, George, you, like your mama, are most welcome here."

"Thank you, ma'am. I've just got back from Northampton County, and I was hopin' to have a word with my ma."

Lizzie joined the conversation, saying calmly, "Anythin' you got to say, George, you can say in front of Eleanor." Eleanor was it? Not Mrs. Edmonds?

Awkwardly, he said, "Edward told me what happened, least ways most of it. I need to hear it from you, and to know you're alright."

"After you left, the Reverend came callin' for you. Seein' as you weren't there, he welcomed himself inside. He said my soul was already damned to hell, so I might as well give in to him. If it hadn't been for Honor...that dog came inside, clean outta the blue, and bit that devil in the arse. While he was distracted, I ran to your granddaddy's."

"Honor never did like the Reverend Kellam much," George said dryly, and Eleanor Edmonds burst out laughing. With that all tension was gone, and Lizzie started guffawing too. She reached across the tea table between them and took Eleanor's hand as the two looked at each other, laughing til the tears rolled. When their crowing finally ceased, the two women quietly sat smiling at each other, and their happiness together made George momentarily content too. He sat for a while longer, occasionally joining the conversation, but mostly watching them until it occurred to him that he was an intruder here.

"Ma, I'm gonna see to this," George said quietly, getting to the point.

Lizzie sighed. "There ain't no need, and nothing good to come of it. Let it be. Let me be."

"Don't know as I can do that."

Eleanor interjected, "George, your mother has landed on her feet, and has the chance to find some peace, finally, in this life."

"Well, whatever happens, it won't affect you, Ma. I'll see to that. Mrs. Edmonds, you have my gratitude for your kindness to my mother."

"George, again, you are always welcome here."

He nodded to his mother, "Be seein' you."

She arose to follow George out, and without another word closed the door behind him. There was, after all, nothing more to say.

As George came up the deerpath to home, Honor at his side, he could smell ham frying. This time when he entered the shack, Honor came too and laid down under the rickety table at George's feet.

"Well, boy?" his grandfather asked.

"Ain't never seen her like that before. I suspect she's gonna stay."

"Yeah, I'd say so. You okay with that?"

George thought about it a minute, and nodded. "I'm gonna head west, so I'm obliged to know that she's gonna be looked after."

Edward arched his eyebrows, "West?"

"Dakota Territory. Gonna get a gold claim if'n I can."

Edward put two plates of ham and fried eggs on the table and sat down across from George on an old stump he'd drug in. George took out his knife to cut his ham, and his grandfather said nonchalantly, "I see that old Bowie knife's held up."

George snorted, "You're just full of surprises, old man."

Edward just chuckled. "That I am. That I am."

"Honor?", George asked, and his grandfather nodded.

"And the mule and Henry rifle too," the old man said smugly.

"Well, you best be takin' Lucky back bein's I'm headin' west."

Edward laughed, "Give 'em to Lem. That mule belonged to Ann." Then the two set to eating their eggs.

Chapter Fifteen

Thursday, May 19, 1882

There are no secrets that time doesn't reveal, although the town of Pungoteague had tried mightily to keep this one from Mamie. The Reverend Kellam had been sharing with all and sundry that he had been accosted by that crazed, wicked Hickman woman, and he only trying to help George. The story went that, out of the goodness of the clergyman's heart, he had made that eight mile trip to Cashville to counsel George not to travel to Franktown. He wanted, you see, to spare the lad the precious time and money such a journey would surely waste. Alas, he was too late, and George had already departed, leaving his maniacal mother behind to fend for herself. The harlot had drug him in the door of the pitiful shack and done her best to have her way with the man of God who, holding tight to his faith in the Lord, had barely managed to fend her off. In her fury at his rejection, she had run off barefoot, wild hair streaming behind her, to God only knows.

Tacitly agreed upon by all, no one mentioned it to Mamie, not even her own family. Not one of them wanted to be the catalyst for what would surely follow. Although Mamie was well loved by the community of Pungoteague, her fearless temper was no secret, and some things were just better left alone. So when Myrtle Custis and Cora Littleton, neighbors gossiping about the sordid tale over the backyard clothesline, looked up to see Mamie standing at the corner of Myrtle's house listening, their flustered attempts to right the wrong simply made matters worse.

"Mamie, oh my goodness, I didn't see you there," Myrtle tried to appear calm, unsure of how much the girl had heard.

"No, I guess you didn't, Miss Myrtle. How 'bout you start at the beginning," the girl said with narrowed, blue eyes.

"The beginning?" Myrtle looked at Cora helplessly, stalling for time. Mamie's mother, Mary, was gonna have their hides.

Cora began, "Now, Mamie, we was just talkin' bout somethin' that happened up near the Maryland line…"

"That ain't the truth, Miss Cora, and you know it well as I do. What I wanna know is when Kellam was at George's farm."

The two women looked at each other, then Myrtle shrugged, saying, "Well, the cat's outta the bag anyway," to Cora. Turning to Mamie, "Wednesday, last week. The day George left for Northampton."

"I see. So everyone knows?"

Guiltily looking at her feet, Cora mumbled, "Pretty much."

"And everyone believes that snake?"

Myrtle Custis drew herself up to her full five feet and two inches, and retorted, "You didn't hear us say that, now did you Mamie? If you caught as much as you're lettin' on, you'd know that we was talkin' bout Lettie Smith."

Mamie nodded. Poor Lettie was the spinster of Pungoteague, nearly thirty years old and still at home, no marriage offers in sight. Not likely to be any either, especially after the lies the good Reverend had spread around about the girl. The story ran along the same lines as that he told of Lizzie Hickman, and when he was done, Lettie's name was sullied permanently in the county of Accomack. The ruined woman went about town with her head down, barely speaking. Much like George, Mamie mused.

While Mamie stood there looking at the sky, hands on her narrow hips, mouth pursed, and thinking, the two older women looked at each other across the clothesline and braced. No tellin' what was gettin' ready to happen.

They almost sighed with relief when Mamie very calmly said, "Miss Cora, go gather the rest of the women and bring 'em here. Don't tell none of the men what's going on."

"Why, Mamie, I don't know what's goin' on."

"I'm goin' home to get Mama. We'll meet you back here." And with that she was gone.

Cora shook her head at Myrtle in disgust, "Well, if this isn't a fine mess you've got me into."

When Mamie came in the front door of the Miller home, she heard raised voices in the kitchen and went to see what the fuss was about. There sat Beelzebub himself calmly at the kitchen table, legs crossed, while her Mama stood, arms folded and silent and her father paced the room.

The clergyman said warmly, the smile not reaching his eyes, "There's the bride now."

"What's the meanin' of this?" Mamie returned in greeting.

When no one spoke up, Mary Miller threw her arms down slapping her hands on her thighs and shared, "Reverend Kellam has decided your weddin' is to be moved up a week. Seems he has a prior engagement that he forgot about til now."

William Miller looked at the floor, refusing to meet his daughter's eye. He only looked up in shock when his youngest girl, a tempest in a teapot, sweetly said, "Well, Mama, we'd better get to work on that dress."

Just after breakfast, Edward had harnessed the horses and headed home to his awaiting farm and his nettled wife, confident now that his grandson had matters in hand. George, Honor at his heel, had set out to call on Lem who never failed to offer his wisdom to any problem with which the young man wrestled. As he crossed the flat fields and briney creeks, he wondered about the new places he would see on his journey west and how different they might be from the only place he'd ever known. His imagination had a hard time calling up any images of the mountains he'd cross, and he couldn't fathom the width of the mighty rivers between himself and Dakota Territory. And trains. He'd never thought to ride a train but that was exactly what he was setting out to do. While still sad that Mamie wouldn't be by his side, a tiny spark of excitement began to grow.

"Honor, we're gonna have us an adventure, boy." The dog wagged his tail in agreement.

Lemuel was sitting on the porch steps when he saw George and his hound. "Welcome home, son!"

"Howdy, Lem."

"How was your time down south?"

When George had finished the saga of his travels, Lem sat pondering for a time. "Seems that trip was worth takin' after all.""

"Yeah, Lem, guess it was."

"Guessin' you've heard about the Reverend's visit to your mama?

George gritted his teeth. "Yeah, Edward was waitin' when I got home."

"What you thinkin' on?"

"Well, old friend, I'm headin' west to Dakota Territory. The only question I got is whether to just head on out or pay a visit to the good Reverend first."

"What you hopin' to gain by payin' that scoundrel a visit?"

"Well, Lemuel, guessin' that's why I'm here. Tryin' to sort this all out. I've been to see Lizzie, and, well, she's happy with Mrs. Edmonds and is gonna stay. I told her that I'd see to Kellam, but she said there weren't no need. Just go on bout my way, and there's a right good part of me wants to do just that."

The old man nodded sagely. "I can see that. Sounds like good advice to me."

"But Lem, there's another part of me that wants to see justice. Wants that fiend to pay for all he's done to me and mine."

"How you gonna go about that?"

This was the point that stumped George every time. "I don't rightly know, I guess. He ain't never gonna admit to it. And if I go to the law, they ain't gonna believe the likes of me. Sugar, I've thought about given' him a good thrashing, but that's sure to land me in a heap of trouble. I keep thinkin' bout David and Goliath, and making the hard decision cause it's the right one. If I walk away, that makes me yellow."

Lemuel laughed out loud, slapping his knee. "Boy, you ain't yellow for walkin' away from a fight you cain't possibly win! I guarantee you, you confront that snake and nothin' but woe will come of it."

"So you thinkin' I should just let it be and head west?"

"Yessir. Not that I ain't gonna miss you, but you got's your whole life waitin' on you."

George nodded, relieved.

"George, there's just one last thing. I was in Pungoteague this mornin' standin' at the back door of the mercantile waitin' on my flour from Mr. Scarborough when that Reverend Kellam came in and announced to him that there's gonna be a weddin' this Saturday."

"Oh yeah?" George asked. Then it dawned on him. "I see."

"Just thought you oughta know is all."

"Thanks, Lem. I'll stop on my way outta town and say goodbye."

Doc Littleton had been in the armchair, feet on a stool and snoring, when his wife, Cora, had rudely whacked him on the arm, handed him his pipe and tobacco pouch, and told him to skedaddle. Still half asleep, he was on the porch, door slammed behind him, before he could gather his wits enough to question what had just occurred. The old man, however, was no fool, and though God might ordain that a wife was to obey her husband in all he said, things ran differently in the Littleton household. So here he sat at the unlit stove in the mercantile, smoking his pipe, and watching near about all the women of Pungateague going in and out of his house.

Coming over to stand by the doctor's chair, Edwin Scarborough said, "Reverend Kellam says there's to be a wedding day after tomorrow."

Doc grunted. "Moved it up, did he?"

"Must be the women are trying to get things sorted right quick for the nuptials."

"Mmhh." His gut told the old codger that something bigger was afoot. Edwin went back to cleaning the counters, and Doc kept watching. When the coast was clear, he headed home.

Mamie sat on her bed, pillow hugged to her belly, and, concentrating, went over the details yet again in her head. Nothing could be left to chance. Too much depended on everyone playing their roles with proper timing. That hypocrite Kellam had unwittingly played right into her hand. The wedding being moved up was not the punishment he intended after all, but a boon, as long as she could pull it all together in time. Her poor mama had worked late into the night, straining her eyes by candlelight, sewing that stupid, blue dress. Of course, Mary knew all about Mamie's plans, was present with all the other women of Pungateague at Cora Littleton's home this afternoon, and the woman had her own role to play in the coming drama. Truth be known, Mary Miller was anticipating her part in Mamie's plan with smug glee. The apple, after all, didn't fall very far from the tree.

George, the warm night spent on top of the buffalo hide, was also going over all the details. Honor lay beside his pallet, running and whimpering in his sleep, chasing rabbits. George too had a plan. Edward, perhaps looking to make up for the years of neglect, had offered to buy his stead, and hold it for him in case he changed his mind and decided to come home. The old man gave him twice what George had paid for it, said he'd keep an eye on the place, but he'd take the chickens and Lucky to Lem's stead for keeping. So Lizzie was safe with Eleanor Edmonds, he had cash for the journey, and the animals would be well tended by his old friend. Not many other loose ends to tie up, far as he could see. Just the one, and he'd see to that on Saturday.

Chapter Sixteen

Saturday, May 21, 1882

Up at the front of the church, standing with the Reverend Kellam, stood poor Josiah Bayly, visibly trembling and looking as white as newly bleached cotton. It hadn't once occurred to Mamie until now that maybe Josiah wasn't too keen on marrying her either. She stood peeking at him and all of the congregation from around the door, not yet ready to make her entrance. Her father, in blessed ignorance, tugged at his collar and hiked up his pants, unaware of the maelstrom to come.

Mamie was dolled up in her new, blue, gingham dress, her hair done up just so with little white flowers artfully inserted here and there. If it weren't for the scowl on her face, William thought she'd be just as pretty as a picture. He absently wondered, pulling yet again at his collar, how long it would take Mamie to forgive him for this. No matter. She would be Josiah's cross to bear after this morning, and he found himself feeling sorry for the boy. Josiah wasn't known to be an assertive lad, and he figured on Mamie running roughshod all over her new husband.

His daughter was still peeping around the door frame when William impatiently asked, "What is it you're lookin' at, girl? Let's get this over and done with!"

"Gotta make sure everyone's here," she said absently, still focused on the pews.

"For the love of God, the whole church is full near to burstin'. There's not a soul on the west side of Accomack County that ain't here today!"

"SSSHHHH! They'll hear you!" she whispered angrily without turning. Thank the Lord above that this was his last daughter.

Finally satisfied, she stepped back from the door, smoothed her skirts, tucked a wisp of hair behind her ear, looked at her father, and said, "I'm ready."

Before she could change her mind, they were in the door, walking down the aisle. The congregation all stood and turned to face the bride-to-be and her father. The men were all smiling at the winsome girl, but the women, their faces told a different tale. If any of the menfolk had been paying the least little bit of attention, they would have seen that each of their wives and daughters shared the same countenance: set, determined, and loaded for bear. Only old Doc Littleton noticed, and a shiver ran up his spine as a goose ran across his grave.

By the time Mamie and William had made it to Josiah at the front of the church, the poor lad looked like his knees were going to give way. As Mamie turned to face Josiah, she caught a movement out of the corner of her eye. Nettie Smith was panicking, pushing her way out of the pew and the church. Nettie was the linchpin of the entire plan and without her this farce of a marriage would proceed. Mamie looked to her mother in terror.

Mary Miller, the eye of all of Mamie's storms, calmly stood up and called to the back of the church, "Oh, Nettie darling! Come sit up here with me won't you?" All eyes turned as one to light on Nettie who stood pinned to the spot like a spooked doe, hand on the door of the church. With no other obvious choice, the poor girl hurried up the aisle, eyes downcast to throw herself down next to Mamie's mother. Mary took the girl's hand and whispered something in her ear, causing Nettie to nod in return. Mamie, stifling a sigh of relief, was turning back to Josiah when a face in the back pew arrested her.

George. She could feel warm tears bubbling up to sting her eyes, but he just smiled at her reassuringly and nodded as if to say, "You can do this, Mamie Miller. I believe in you." She lifted her chin, nodding too. Yes, I can. Lord above but his courage near about broke her heart.

The Reverend began intoning words, but Mamie wasn't really listening. She was waiting. Any second...but Nettie sat silently next to Mary, saying not a word. No, no, no! Too long! She was taking too long! Mamie wanted to look back over her shoulder at Nettie, but she didn't dare. If it went on too much longer though, she'd be wed to Josiah Bayly! What was happening?

Then, "If anyone has a reason to object to this..."

"I object!"

Stunned, Mamie turned to see George standing in the aisle at the back of the church, everyone turned to him expectantly as if they'd been waiting for this to happen.

George walked forward a step, saying, "I object, but not to the marriage of Mamie Miller and Josiah Bayly." What?

"I don't object to this marriage. I've always known Mamie Miller was too good for the likes of me. I want her to be happy, have a family, and live a good life. I want her to have what I can't. It's you I object to, Reverend Kellam, you and your evil ways. I object to the sinful way in which you've treated me all my life, the hatred you've shown me in so many ways. You made it your goal to turn the entire county against me, workin' tirelessly til you reached that goal. You made me feel like I wasn't fit to wipe your boots on." Not a soul stirred, the shame of George's truth rooting them to the spot.

"I object to what you did to my mother, and the lies you told bout her. I don't expect none to believe me when I say that it was you who attacked her, but it is still the truth. I know it and you know it. Everybody else is gonna have to decide whether or not they know it."

The Reverend Kellam was apoplectic with rage, face redder than a tomato, a vein pulsing on the side of his head. He looked down to William Miller, hissing, "Get that miscreant out of here!" William didn't move.

"I know it." Nettie's small voice could barely be heard until Mary squeezed her hand in encouragement. She said louder, now standing up tall, eyes on the clergyman, "I know it. I know it's the truth what you did to Lizzie Hickman cause you done it to me too!"

Kellam boomed, "Nettie Smith, sit down! Enough of these lies!"

But then other women started to stand up too. Cora Littleton said loudly, "I know it too," and Doc Littleton looked up in appalled shock at his wife.

There was a ruckus now in the church, murmuring, whispering, shuffling, and the Reverend realized he had lost control of the situation completely. "We must finish this ceremony, good people of Pungoteague, and then we can calmly discuss these misunderstandings," he tried to reason.

But then it was William Miller standing up. "We will not be finishing this ceremony, Reverend Kellam. I object to this marriage!" Beside her, Josiah Bayly nearly collapsed with relief.

Trying to appease the weathered sailor, Kellam placatingly said, "William, you don't mean that surely. You know this is what's best for your girl."

"You talked until you was blue in the face trying to convince me of that, and I am ashamed to admit that I went along cause I was scared of you and of God. But I see now you weren't speakin' for God, now were ya? And you sure weren't spreading the good Lord's word when you were assailin' these womenfolk!"

"But William, I did no such thing!"

A frighteningly calm voice said from one of the middle pews, "Get out." Everyone craned their necks to see who had spoken, and then Doc Littleton stood up. "Get out, Kellam." Then all the men were on their feet, the rage in their eyes undeniable, and suddenly Kellam feared for life and limb. Doc didn't need to say it a third time for the clergyman fled, leaving his bible on the podium.

The next to flee was Josiah Bayly. Having come within a hair's breadth of catastrophe, he got while the gettin' was good. Mamie ran to her father, hugging him hard. When she let go, her mama was still holding Nettie's hand smiling, and, oddly, so was Nettie.

"Thank you, Mamie." Mamie looked at her confused, so Nettie continued, "You've set me free."

"Today, Nettie, we've all been freed," Mary Miller said pointedly.

Standing on her tiptoes, Mamie looked for George, sure that he must be makin' his way to the front of the church to her. There'd be nothing standing between them now. She pushed her way through the oddly joyous crowd towards the back of the church, but when she got to the door, she still hadn't found him.

Outside, through the backwoods of Accomack County, George was walking west.

Afterword

      This book has been over a year in the making. The idea first took hold of my imagination when I was diligently working on my little acorn of a tree through Ancestry.com. I was fascinated when I stumbled upon my second great grandfather who happened to have his mother's surname. Delving deeper, I discovered that she had never been married, that she had borne her only child early in life, and that she spent the remainder of her life unwed. The common belief amongst all the learned Eastern of Shore of Virginia historians is that Benjamin Upshur Doughty was the father of illegitimate George Davis Hickman. What is known for sure is that both Elizabeth 'Lizzie' Hickman and Benjamin were under the employ of Benjamin Wise, a 36 year old farmer, at the time of George's conception. It's all there in black and white on the 1860 federal census. Lizzie then pops up again twenty years later, again in the federal census, as a widowed housekeeper. We can follow her life through these documents until her death in 1912 when she's interred in Hollies Baptist Cemetery, Keller, Accomack, Virginia.

      Presto! A skeletal beginning to my story. I had the bones, and my imagination started to supply the flesh. I'd been studying the history of the 1800's, especially in reference to the Eastern Shore of Virginia, so it wasn't hard to guess why Lizzie would need to lie about her marital status and claim widowhood. Further, Benjamin Upshur Doughty not being listed as George's father on his death certificate came as little surprise. Instead, one Edward Hickman, politically correct surname and suspiciously the name of George's maternal grandfather, filled in the blank space. But then the information was supplied by John Thomas Hickman, George's son who may never have learned the truth.

      At that time in our history, the church could be considered law as much as the government, and so the teachings of a rigid faith would have made the young woman and her bastard son pariahs to the God fearing community in which they resided. When, even now, we can see all around us the evidence of bigotry and judgment, I can only imagine what life must have been like for the two of them. The flesh of their story grew. At every twist and turn, their struggle took shape as I envisioned Lizzie and George's struggle to simply survive.

      Elizabeth Hickman, her son George, and all the other Hickmans are based upon real people, real history, and my vivid imagination. I conjured the flesh that covered the bones. Benjamin Doughty and his family members are factual as well, although their personalities, hopes, and dreams are as lost to history as the proof of George's paternity. The other names belong to fictional characters, although their surnames are often plucked from the long lines that traverse the more than four hundred years of Eastern Shore history. Yet, here and there, throughout the story interesting facts arise. I did my homework. Cassatt was really on the Eastern Shore planning for the PRR's move south, the flora and fauna are true to the region, and buffalo hides really sold for $2.50. The rest is my very vivid, very tenacious imagination.

Lightning Source UK Ltd.
Milton Keynes UK
UKHW050051011222
413021UK00030B/192